R

TRIBUTE BRIDES OF THE DREXIAN WARRIORS #4

TANA STONE

BROADMOOR BOOKS

CHAPTER ONE

Torven leaned against the weathered bar and eyed the green-skinned Grindul pouring drinks behind it. He'd been to enough seedy outposts to know when his drinks were being watered down. He glanced around the dimly lit room and tried not to inhale the smoke that hung in the air like a thick haze. This place was as seedy as they came.

"Noovian whiskey," he said, holding the alien's gaze. "Straight."

The heavyset bartender grunted, but he seemed to size up Torven's build and the similar bulk of his Drexian shipmate, his eyes flicking to the Inferno Force insignia on their uniforms before nodding. If the Drexian uniform didn't scare people, the flame insignia that represented the warrior race's elite fighting force did. The Drexian Empire may have been known throughout the galaxy as a race of warriors who defended those weaker than themselves, but their elite Inferno Force was the team known for enforcing their might with equal parts justice and fury.

Inferno Force warriors were rough and battle-scarred, and spent most of their time fighting on the outskirts of the galaxy. They weren't a usual sight at this particular trading outpost, but one look at their tattoos and longer hair, and the various aliens in the bar had given them a wide berth.

The bartender poured a generous amount of green liquid into a glass and slid it over to Torven.

"Scaring the locals again?" Torven's best friend asked, as he thumped a hand on his broad back.

Torven picked up his drink and tossed it back in one gulp, feeling the whisky burn on the way down. He turned to Dakar. Even though his friend was tall, as were all Drexians, he still had several inches on him. "No trouble this time, my friend."

Dakar cocked an eyebrow. "You haven't even met her, and you're already on your best behavior. I'm impressed." He eyed Torven's face. "Now, if we could only get you cleaned up a bit."

"There will be time before we arrive on the station." Torven stroked a hand down his stubbly chin and brushed a strand of dark hair off his forehead. "Until then, I want others to know I'm Inferno Force. It keeps the local troublemakers in check."

Dakar's gaze dropped to the thick, black lines under his friend's eyes. "I don't think that's a secret."

Originally worn by Inferno Force before battles, some of the warriors had permanently adopted the markings as a warning to any they encountered. Considering the way creatures in the bar had flinched when the two massive Drexians had entered, it seemed to work.

"You promised no fights during our journey," Dakar reminded him.

"You know I never pick fights. I only right wrongs."

"I know, my friend. There is no more honorable Drexian than you." Dakar picked up his own glass and swirled the liquid. "Your high standards do seem to get us into more than a few fights, though."

Torven raised his empty glass in salute. "The price to pay for doing what's right."

His friend took a long gulp. "Who's going to keep us in check while you're romancing your new bride?"

Torven leaned back against the bar, thinking of the tribute bride he'd be meeting in a few days' time. Even though he'd seen her image, he knew little about the human female chosen for him. Like almost all Drexians, his name was in a lottery for one of the human brides, since female babies on his world had become a rare occurrence.

Instead of allowing their race to die out when they realized the birthing trend, the Drexians had scoured the universe for compatible species and had happened upon Earth. Even though Earthlings had some physical differences, about half of the females had enough genetic similarities to make them suitable for mating.

After waiting for years, Torven's name had been chosen for the next available human mate. From the image he'd been staring at since he'd gotten the notification, he knew she had pale, wavy hair, and blue eyes. And he knew what he'd already known about all human females—they were small in comparison and had only two breasts, and no arousal nodes down their spine. What had been a surprise was the jolt of familiarity he'd felt when he'd first seen her face on the screen. He knew it was impossible, but he felt like he already knew this female. Even her image stirred his blood in a way he'd never experienced before.

"I'll be back before you know it," Torven said, tapping the edge of his glass for more whiskey.

Dakar gave a snort of disbelief and ran a hand through his own shaggy, brown hair before pulling it up and fastening it into a knot on the top of his head. "I doubt that. You're lucky, though. I hear they've halted transport of humans until the High Command is sure our enemy won't attack them. They don't want to risk the females."

Torven's temper flared as he thought about the Kronock, the Drexian's sworn enemy, and violent creatures known for invading and wiping out entire species. As a member of Inferno Force, he'd been fighting them on the outskirts for years, holding them back, and protecting the solar system that contained Earth. When the Kronock had attempted to invade Earth over thirty years earlier, the Drexians had stopped them, discovering that humans were compatible with their species in the process. The governments on Earth made a deal with the Drexians—protection from the Kronock in exchange for human mates. It had worked well—the Kronock had been held at bay and Earth had been saved.

However, only recently, his people had discovered that the Kronock had been hiding their technological advancements and were planning a massive invasion of Earth. The recent incursions had been the reason he'd been unable to join his waiting bride until now. He couldn't abandon his shipmates in the middle of a battle. Even now, part of him felt guilty taking leave.

"Maybe I should wait until after we've defeated them once and for all," Torven said. "Inferno Force needs every warrior."

Dakar shook his head. "This war may never end. If you don't claim your bride, someone else will."

Even though he'd never met her, he'd been staring at his mate's image for weeks, and already thought of her as his. The idea of her with another Drexian made him clench his fists.

Dakar laughed. "Don't worry, Torv. As soon as our shuttle is refueled, we'll get out of this dump and head for the station."

Torven slammed back the whiskey the bartender poured him and glanced around the dive bar. He supposed this outpost was as good as any for fuel and supplies, and it was located halfway between his fleet and the space station where he'd meet his bride, but he also knew it attracted smugglers and arms dealers and all sorts of lowlifes. He watched as heads huddled together at the bar and money was passed underneath tables in dark corners. Even the air he breathed was tainted with sour-smelling smoke as patrons used bubbling inhalers to get their high. The sooner they left, the better.

"What about you?" he asked his friend. "You on the list for a bride?"

"I'm on there, somewhere." Dakar shrugged. "I'm a third son, so I won't come up for a while."

Torven nodded. He knew one of the reasons he'd finally been matched was because he was an only son. He would be the only male to carry on his family's name. Although he wasn't a member of the elite class, he was descended from a long line of valiant warriors. It was no secret that brides went first to the elite families, and then to only sons. Third sons like Dakar would be farther down the list, although knowing his friend, Torven didn't think he much cared.

Dakar had a reputation throughout the galaxy for being able to sweet talk any female out of her clothes in a matter of minutes. He was famous on the pleasure planets, and infamous among males of all species wishing to keep their females away from his irresistible charms.

"You could become a captain and move up the list," Torven said, taking the refilled glass from the bartender. "Our commander didn't even put himself on the list and was called away because he got matched."

Dakar choked on his laughter. "Don't worry about me, Torv. And wasn't Commander Dorn practically dragged off his ship? I pity the female who got matched with that battle-hardened warrior."

Torven allowed himself a smile. He, too, remembered the stormy look on their commander's face when he'd had to leave the fleet and report to the Boat, the space station where tribute brides were housed. "It will be good to see him."

Dakar nudged him. "You'll have to tell me all about the Earthlings. And the fantasy suites. Now those I would like to see"

Torven's face warmed. "I'll bet you would." Even though he'd never seen the space station, the stories about it were legendary. It had been designed with human pleasure in mind, and contained everything human females loved most. He had no idea what those things were, but he knew the station was nothing like the old battle cruiser he'd come from. He only hoped he wasn't a shock to his bride.

He rubbed a hand across the scruff on his cheeks. Warriors in Inferno Force battled in the farthest regions of space, so they were allowed to be rougher around the edges. Torven wondered if he should try to appear less wild for the Earthling, like Dakar had suggested. As he debated the possibility of being clean-shaven for the first time in years, he heard a commotion from the entrance to the bar.

Murmurs passed through the crowd as a group of uniformed Drexians entered—these warriors with close-cropped hair and starched uniforms—and many patrons drifted away, as the heavy boots clomped across the floor. The green-skinned bartender disappeared, as the four warriors approached Dakar and Torven.

Dakar raised an eyebrow and muttered under his breath. "And I thought *we* weren't welcome."

The lead Drexian soldier looked both men up and down when he reached them. "Torven of House Kantar?"

Torven shifted his eyes to his friend before answering. "Yes?"

"Your presence is requested by the High Command."

"I know," Torven said. "We're on our way to the Boat. This is just a quick stop for refueling."

"It's a long trip," Dakar added with a grin.

The other Drexian didn't smile or acknowledge Dakar. "You need to come with us."

A suspicious tingle ran down Torven's spine. He'd sent word to the space station that he was en route. Why send a squad to intercept him? They knew he was traveling with Dakar so his friend and crewmate could pilot the shuttle back to Inferno Force. "What's all this about?"

The Drexian Crossed his arms in front of his chest. "We are here to bring you in for questioning."

Dakar held up his hands. "Whoa. Questioning for what? This guy's on his way to the Boat to be matched with a tribute bride."

"Not anymore, he's not." The lead Drexian let his eyes slide over to Dakar before returning to Torven. "He's wanted for questioning in a criminal matter."

"A criminal matter?" Torven gave a small shake of his head. "I think you have the wrong Drexian."

"Negative." The warrior clamped an iron cuff around his wrists before Torven could react. "You, Torven of House Kantar, are being charged with treason and conspiring with the enemy."

Torven's mouth dropped open as he stared at the shackles on his hands. He heard his friend protesting loudly in the background, but all he could think about was the pretty blonde who would never be his.

CHAPTER TWO

Trista sighed as she slipped out of the suite, letting the doors slide closed on the loud festivities within, and feeling relieved to be in the relative quiet of the corridor. She could still hear the music pounding and the peals of laughter, but she was glad to be by herself.

"Macarena!" someone screamed from inside, and Trista shook her head. Yep, she'd escaped just in time.

The surprise wedding had evolved from a pretty ceremony overlooking the African savannah (courtesy of alien holographic technology) to a dance party that would probably go until late in the night, if the Palaxian booze had anything to say about it. Her feet, which she'd jammed into high-heeled stripy sandals for the party, already ached.

It wasn't that she didn't enjoy celebrating with the other tribute brides on the space station. All the other Earth women were great, but if she was being honest, Trista felt like she didn't belong.

She glanced down at the simple yellow sundress she had on. She'd much rather be wearing jeans and a loose-fit T-shirt, and the second she got back to her suite, she was losing the dress and heels. Not to mention the makeup the tribute bride liaison, Reina, had put on her. She knew tribute brides were supposed to look a certain way, but when she looked in the mirror and saw her usually wavy blonde hair blown stick straight, and her blue eyes heavily made up, she saw a stranger.

Breathing in the cool night air, Trista stopped along the wooden pathway and looked out over the holographic environment. Even though the savannah was dark, she could hear the sounds of animals and the rustling of tall grass in the breeze. The alien technology that created all of it was pretty amazing, but it was another stark reminder that she was out of her league.

What would the other tribute brides say if they knew what she was really like? They seemed pretty accepting—they'd adapted to living with aliens, after all—but what would they think if they knew about her past? Her new friends on the space station included a former ballerina, an Instagram influencer, and a reporter. That was a far cry from dating members of a motorcycle club and not even holding down a real job, unless you counted working on the broken bikes for no pay.

A bird cawed loudly as it swooped overhead, and Trista jumped. Even though the aliens had cleaned her up pretty well and given her an entirely new wardrobe containing nothing black or leather, she felt like she was living a lie. Not that she wasn't grateful for being rescued from her crappy former life. Being taken from Earth was the best thing that had ever happened to her, especially since she'd been running from a particularly bad ex-boyfriend. She shuddered even thinking about Rick and his nasty temper. No, she was glad to be far away on a space station. She was just tired.

She sighed as she slipped off her shoes and hooked her index finger through the heel straps to carry them. Tired from the party, but also from trying to pretend she belonged, when deep down, she knew she was a complete fraud.

Technically, none of the Earthlings belonged. They'd all been taken from Earth by the Drexians—huge, brawny alien warriors with bronze skin and muscles for days. Guys who would have been way out of her league back on Earth, Trista's little voice reminded her.

The Drexians were smart about taking women, she'd give them that. They only took a few at a time. Plus, the chosen women had to be one-hundred-percent compatible with Drexians—not all were—and have few family and friends to miss them.

"That would be me," Trista muttered to herself, as she padded in her bare feet along the wooden walkway toward the inclinator.

She'd been taken from Earth and brought up to the Boat, the high-tech space station that resided behind Saturn and housed all the tribute brides, as well as other aliens who kept the operation running. That had been a few weeks ago. The other two brides she'd been brought up with, who'd become her friends, were already mated to their guys. She still waited.

If she was being completely honest with herself, Trista hoped her Drexian never arrived. She couldn't bear to see his disappointment when he saw that he'd been matched to someone who wasn't beautiful or hard-bodied or glamorous. She touched a hand to her hair, remembering that her stepfather had always called it dishwater blonde, and made a face. Who wanted that?

Trista could imagine how a big, alpha, Drexian warrior would react if she told him she hated wearing dresses and liked working on engines. The Drexians tried to make all the tribute brides happy, but she doubted they would let her tinker with their spaceships. That would go over like a lead balloon. No, she'd rather stay in her perpetual holding pattern on the station, than have her Drexian realize he'd gotten a D-list bride.

Not that waiting on the Boat was a hardship. The station had been designed for the sole purpose of enticing human women and making the process of being taken from Earth and paired with an alien mate more palatable. The Drexians and the other aliens who had designed the station had taken inspiration from Earth movies and TV, and had even nicknamed the station after the show *The Love Boat.*

Trista laughed to herself as she walked, thinking of the dated television that had inspired the station. The influence of the 70s and 80s could be seen in everything from the decor to the fashion, not that it bothered her much. She reached an arched doorway and swiped her hand across a panel. When the doors swished open, she stepped onto the inclinator—like an elevator that could go sideways as well as up and down—and heard the 80s Muzak piped in overhead.

She hummed along with "Take on Me" as the sleek, white compartment surged up, the uplighting giving the walls a lavender hue. Her suite was only one floor above, on the Greek Isles wing, and as she stepped out of the inclinator, she saw the familiar, whitewashed buildings clinging to the side of the hill that dropped into the sea.

Of course, it wasn't actually a Greek island, but the Drexians had such sophisticated holographic technology that it not only looked like one, it smelled and sounded like one. Trista breathed in the scent of saltwater, and heard the waves slapping the sides of the fishing boats in the harbor.

Each tribute bride was placed in a holographic fantasy suite designed to look like an idyllic setting—from a South Pacific overwater bungalow, to a ski chalet, to a safari suite on the African savannah. Somehow, they'd known that this mix of bright-white houses topped with blue domes, and pink flowers spilling down the mountain, was her dream vacation—a place she'd never imagined she'd ever see when she was stuck back in a small town in the middle of nowhere.

She walked up the wide, whitewashed stairs until she reached another arched doorway, and waved her hand across a flat panel.

"Trista!" the voice from behind made her pause and cringe.

She'd been so close. Turning, she smiled at the tall, willowy woman with light-gray skin, and a shock of blue hair that curled straight up from her head. "Reina, I thought you were still at the party."

"The wedding, you mean," Reina said, giggling. "Can you believe those two managed to plan a surprise wedding that even Serge didn't know about?"

The doors to her suite glided open, and Trista looked longingly inside. "How is Serge? Did he recover from the shock?"

Reina tapped a spindly finger on her chin. "It may take him a while to get over the disappointment of not getting to plan a splashy wedding. He *is* a wedding planner at heart. Luckily, he's got your wedding to distract him."

Trista's stomach did a series of flips at the thought of her wedding. The Drexian warrior she'd been matched with was a part of their elite Inferno Force, and had been delayed battling the enemy on the outskirts of space. "I'd have to have a groom to plan a wedding."

Reina hooked an arm through hers, and walked them both inside the suite. "Like that's stopped Serge before."

Trista knew that was true. The pint-sized wedding planner—from an alien species called Gatazoid—was a force of nature when it came to planning. She'd seen how he'd pulled together weddings for the other tributes, sometimes in a matter of days.

"Have you given any more thought to what you'd like for your wedding?" Reina asked as she crossed the living room, her heels clicking against the polished white floors, and opened the sliding-glass door that led onto a balcony.

Trista sank onto one of the white, slipcovered sofas as her pulse quickened. The last thing she wanted to think about was a wedding, especially since she'd never laid eyes on the man she was supposed to marry. She knew she could opt not to be mated to him, but then she'd have to go live with the few humans who'd rejected their matches on the other side of the station. There was no returning to Earth once you'd been taken.

Part of her thought that she could learn to like anyone, especially since all the Drexians seemed to be gorgeous and built. Another part of her knew that there were some things she could never live with again. Things she'd promised herself she'd never tolerate.

"Trista?" Reina asked. "Your wedding?"

"What? No, I haven't really thought about it," Trista told the Vexling, as she came back inside and took the chair across from her. "I wasn't the type of girl who grew up daydreaming about a fancy wedding."

Reina cocked her head. "I thought all Earth females wanted huge weddings. Don't you all want to 'say yes to the dress?'"

Trista thought about her ex-boyfriend, and how all she'd wanted was to get so far away from him he'd never be able to find her. Her heart raced, and her mouth went dry. Even though she knew now he could never get to her, the fear still clawed at her. She inhaled deeply to steady her breath and managed a smile. "Don't believe everything you see on TV."

"You look a little green, hon," Reina said. "Did you drink too much at the wedding?"

Trista gave an abrupt shake of her head as she pushed bad memories from her mind and took a couple of deep breaths to help her heart rate return to normal. "I'm fine."

Reina stood and crossed to the wooden sideboard against one of the whitewashed cave walls, pouring a glass of water from the carafe. "If we're going to take you dress shopping tomorrow, you need to be feeling your best."

"Dress shopping?" Trista took the glass and gratefully sipped the cool water.

"Regardless of what type of wedding you have, you'll need a dress. Even Katie with her surprise wedding had a dress."

Trista drained the glass and set it on the wooden coffee table. "Dresses don't look good on me."

"What do you mean? If I understand Earth phrases correctly, you have an hourglass figure. You'd look lovely in just about any design."

Trista heard herself repeating phrases her ex-boyfriend had

hammered into her psyche. "I've got thighs like tree trunks, and my boobs aren't perky enough."

"Perky enough for what?" Reina eyed her. "Earth trees must be very small, if your legs are the size of their trunks."

"I'm not like the other girls," Trista said, hearing her voice crack.

"No," Reina said. "Your hair is light, and your eyes are very blue. Is this not desirable on Earth? I thought some males liked yellow hair."

Trista shrugged. "Not my kind of blonde." She waved a hand over her nose. "And I have freckles."

Reina squinted at her. "Those pale dots? Are those not desirable, either?"

"They're not exactly sexy. At least I've never been told they were."

Reina stood and joined her on the couch. "I think someone told you these things, and you chose to believe them." She patted her hand. "You would not have been chosen as a tribute bride if you were not deemed desirable."

"That doesn't mean my Drexian will like them," Trista said, giving voice to her fear.

"I think any Drexian would be pleased to be mated with you." Reina squeezed her hand. "You worry too much. I'm sure once your Drexian warrior arrives, everything will be perfect. You'll see."

Trista let out a long breath. Maybe Reina was right. She needed to stop worrying and leave her past behind her, once and for all. But that was easier said than done.

A pounding on the door made both women turn. Reina hurried over and opened it, letting Serge practically fall into the room.

The small alien wore a mango-orange suit with wide lapels and flared pants, and his matching platform boots gave him the extra inches needed to reach Reina's waist. His purple hair was spiked and flushing pink from the roots as he waved his hands in the air.

"This is a catastrophe," he said, as he began pacing.

"What's happened?" Reina asked. "I thought you were at Katie's wedding."

Serge paused. "You mean the wedding they planned without me? That's a topic for another day, let me tell you." He waved his hands more and resumed pacing. "No, this is about Torven."

"Torven?" Trista repeated the word. "That sounds familiar."

"It should," Serge said. "It's the name of your fiancé."

Reina put a hand to her mouth. "Don't tell me he was killed. I don't know if I can handle another Drexian mate being killed in battle before he reaches the Boat."

"Worse," Serge said, his voice dropping, as if he were afraid of them being overheard.

Trista's stomach clenched, both at the thought of the fiancé she'd never met, and at the prospect that something worse than death had happened. "What could be worse than being killed in battle?"

"For a Drexian warrior, being arrested for treason," Serge said. "He's being brought here to appear before the High Command."

"Treason?" Trista collapsed onto the couch. So much for everything being perfect when her Drexian arrived. "And he's coming here? When?"

"Now."

CHAPTER THREE

Torven's mind whirled as he sat on the transport ship, his hands manacled together in front of him. A pair of Drexian guards sat on either side of him, and another stood at the door to the ship's cockpit. The engines rumbled beneath his feet as they flew toward the space station.

How had this happened? He was still heading to the Boat, but now he was going as a prisoner accused of treason. He still couldn't believe the charges, and his pulse raced the more he thought about it.

Treason? Even the word was like bile in his mouth. He could never imagine betraying his people in any way, much less by conspiring with the enemy. He'd spent most of his life fighting the Kronock. The idea of working with them was as foreign to him as breathing underwater.

He shook his head and one of the guards looked suspiciously over at him. No. They had the wrong Drexian. This was all a mistake. As soon as he talked to the High Command, he would make them see that.

Torven lifted his shackled hands and wiped a trickle of sweat off his brow. The more he focused on the false accusations, the angrier he became, and the faster his heart beat. He was surprised the guard at the door couldn't hear the pounding from across the room.

At that moment, the door slid open, and the guard stepped to one side. A Drexian in a crisp uniform stepped into the room holding an electronic tablet, only looking up when the door shut behind him.

"We'll be arriving at the station shortly," the man said, meeting Torven's eyes.

Torven did not recognize this man from the bar. "And you are?"

"Your counsel."

"Counsel?" Torven shifted on the hard, metal bench.

"Any accused is allowed counsel before they appear before High Command." The man rocked back on his heels. "I'm here to explain the charges and the evidence."

"There can't be any evidence. I didn't do it."

The man nodded, as if he'd heard that before. "Even so, you've been charged with serious crimes. That doesn't happen without evidence."

Torven's clenched his fists. "I'm telling you it's not true. I never conspired with anyone, much less the filthy Kronock." He jerked his hands, awkwardly pointing at the roof of the ship. "Who do you think has been battling them out there?"

The man flinched, looking back down at the tablet and swiping his finger across it. "Are you saying you didn't send transmissions to the enemy, telling them how to breech our defenses of the Boat?"

Torven started to leap to his feet, but the guards next to him held him back. "Of course not. Why would I do that?"

"Maybe for the credits that appeared in your personal accounts yesterday?"

"What?" Torven gave a brusque shake of his head. "I don't know anything about that."

His counsel let out a sigh. "So, someone put credits in your account for no reason?"

"I'm sure they had a reason. To set me up." Torven tried to

steady his breathing. "If I was really a traitor, don't you think I'd be better at it? Why would I do all these things you say I've done, and make it so easy to trace them back to me?"

"I think some would argue you didn't expect to get caught, or you didn't think anyone would notice."

Torven narrowed his eyes. "Who did notice? It sounds like someone had to know what they were looking for. Maybe you should be talking to that person."

"I can't disclose how the information was brought to the High Command, but be assured they were acting on information from a trusted source."

Torven sank back. He knew what that meant. Someone more important or more elite than him had tipped off the High Command, although he couldn't imagine who hated him enough to do this. As far as he knew, he didn't have any enemies. At least not among his Drexian brothers. He knew without a doubt that no one on Inferno Force would betray him. It had to have come from higher up.

His stomach tightened. That meant that his appearance in front of the High Command was no more than a formality. He couldn't prove his innocence, if he couldn't challenge his accuser.

The ship slowed, and his Drexian defender took a step to right himself. Although Torven couldn't see outside, he suspected they were approaching the space station as the engines shifted and the floor shook. He'd been on ships long enough to recognize the feel of a vessel preparing to land.

"When will I appear in front of High Command?" Torven asked. He still had the grime of the trip and the dingy outpost bar on him, and he'd rather not appear in a wrinkled uniform and with a face full of stubble. He doubted that what was acceptable among the battle-hardened warriors in Inferno Force would fly with the elite rulers of High Command.

"Almost immediately." The man's eyes flicked to Torven's uniform. "Although I can request a chance for you to change."

"Thank you." Torven wanted to throttle the Drexian, but he also knew his counsel was probably the only shot he had at proving his innocence.

With a curt nod, the man left the room as the ship jolted and the engines powered down. The guards hoisted him to his feet, and marched him out of the holding room and down the ship's ramp.

Torven tilted his head back as he got his first glimpse of the space station formally called the Love Boat. Even though he knew it was only the hangar bay, he was surprised that it looked similar to every other one he'd seen. Lots of gray metal, high ceilings with exposed steel beams, and ships of various sizes lined up across an expansive floor.

He noticed eyes on him, and he straightened up to his full height and threw back his shoulders. No way was he going to act like the traitor they thought he was. He knew he was a loyal Drexian warrior, and that was how he was going to act.

They exited the hangar bay, and the corridors became sleek and white with curved walls. Windows looking out into space ran along one side, and Torven couldn't help but look longingly at the stars dotting the blackness. Would this be his last glimpse of the outside world? He didn't know how hearings for treason went, because he'd never heard of a Drexian committing treason. His face burned with the reminder that he was being accused of betraying his people.

"Torven." The booming voice made him look up. His old Commander was striding toward him, making others scurry out of his path.

"Commander Dorn." He attempted to cross a fist to his heart in salute, but his shackled hands made it impossible.

Dorn scowled at the metal around his wrists and cut his eyes to the guards. "Take those off him."

The guards hesitated. "He's being transported to appear before the High Command."

"I know where he's going. I am a member of the High Command." Dorn's bright-green eyes flashed. "This man is a member of Inferno Force and a loyal Drexian. He does not deserve to be dragged through the station like a criminal."

The guards fumbled with the shackles as they unhooked them. Torven rubbed his wrists as he met Dorn's gaze. "Thank you."

Dorn clapped a hand on his shoulder. "I don't know what's going on, but I know you are no traitor. I refuse to believe any member of Inferno Force would ever betray his brothers."

"Never," Torven said solemnly.

Dorn nodded, as if Torven's word was all the confirmation he needed.

"I know nothing of these transmissions they claim I made, or of the credits that appeared in my account." Torven kept his voice low as people passed by. "Someone wants it to look like I've done things I haven't."

Dorn took his arm and pulled him out of earshot of the guards. "There is someone within the Drexian Empire who is conspiring with our enemy. I don't know why or who, but I know it reaches the highest level."

Torven angled his head. "Are you telling me the High Command is compromised?"

"Yes, but I have been unable to determine who it is." Dorn let out an impatient breath. "As you can imagine, I cannot make accusations without being sure."

"Even though you are one of the elite class?"

Dorn gave a mirthless laugh. "Don't remind me."

Torven's heart began to pound. If this man had to tread lightly, what hope was there for a warrior who wasn't one of the privileged?

"So how do I prove my innocence?" he asked.

Dorn's face contorted. "I don't know if we can. Not yet, at least." He gripped Torven's arm. "My brother and I are working as quickly and covertly as we can, but this is buried deep."

"Are you saying I'll be convicted of treason?" His mouth went dry. "The penalty is death."

Dorn's eyes dropped to Torven's hands. "We need more time."

Torven's breath hitched in his throat, as he realized the message his former commander was sending him. He needed to give them a chance to prove his innocence by doing something that was completely against everything he'd ever been taught.

He needed to run.

Torven met Dorn's eyes, and he gave an almost imperceptible nod. Then his gaze slid past the Drexian to the woman walking along the corridor, and all the air rushed out of him. Her blue eyes widened as she saw him, and he knew instantly it was the woman from the picture that he'd been looking at for weeks.

Trista, the tribute bride he'd been matched with and the woman he'd been thinking about since he'd first seen her image, was staring at him like she'd seen a ghost.

CHAPTER FOUR

Trista knew her mouth was dangling open, but she couldn't help it. Was this really Torven, the Drexian warrior she'd been matched with? She knew Drexians were big and brawny, and every one she'd seen so far was gorgeous, but she hadn't expected this.

She blinked a few times as she stared at him from across the corridor. His dark uniform was rumpled, and his chocolate-brown hair tousled, but what struck her most was how dangerous he looked. The jacket of his uniform hung open—almost as if it had been ripped open in a scuffle— exposing a leather cord around his throat that had what looked like a massive, ebony shark's tooth hanging from it. Dark stubble covered his face, and his gold eyes were lined in black. He looked every bit the criminal she'd been told he was, and she took a small step back.

Trista knew a bad boy when she spotted one, and this guy was trouble, with a capital *T*. Which explained why her hands were clammy, and all the blood had raced to her lower body.

"We shouldn't be here," she said to Reina, who'd gone mute beside her.

The Vexling nodded, and put a hand on Trista's elbow to steer her away. "The next time you insist on something, remind me not to listen to you."

Trista knew her liaison was right. The only reason they were standing in the corridor near the hangar bay was because she'd insisted. Now that she thought about it, Trista wasn't sure why it had been so important she get a glimpse of him in person. Curiosity?

Reina had been against it, claiming there was no good reason to see him, since she would be matched with another warrior once Torven was convicted. According to Reina's sources, the evidence against him was significant, and a conviction was all but guaranteed.

After repeating his name in her head for weeks, Trista couldn't let him go so easily. Even if she ended up with someone else, she felt the need to see him and know what might have been. Now, looking at him, she knew Reina had been right. She shouldn't have come.

She instinctively glanced down at the jeans and black T-shirt she'd thrown on, and wished she'd chosen something else. Why did she suddenly care what she looked like? It wasn't like she'd ever see him again, and it didn't matter what he thought about her, even though part of her wished she'd tried to look more feminine. Strangely, she didn't want this convict and complete stranger to be disappointed with her.

Snap out of it, she told herself as she willed herself to move. You don't need to impress him.

Torven's eyes held hers, and her pulse fluttered. She had an urge to shake herself, and at the same time run away screaming, but her feet were like lead.

Not again, she thought, as she groaned inwardly. What was it about bad boys that had always attracted her? It had never ended well in the past, but that clearly didn't stop her from practically gaping at the towering warrior who would have looked at home in any biker bar on Earth.

Reina tugged at her arm and she took a step, her eyes never leaving Torven.

"You're my mate." His voice was a low rumble echoing in her bones.

Reina made a small squeaking noise, and Trista could sympathize. Something about his tone made her feel like a mouse caught in a trap. She couldn't move away from him, even though she knew she should.

"Trista," Reina pulled her, her voice insistent. "We should go."

Torven's eyes drifted briefly to the Vexling, before returning to her. "Trista from Iowa."

Her name sounded exotic the way he pronounced each syllable slowly, and with emphasis. He even made the word "Iowa" sound more interesting.

Before she could let Reina drag her away, Torven had crossed the corridor to stand inches away from her. The guards around him reached for their blasters, but Dorn ordered them to stand down.

Reina did not release her arm, but tightened her grip. Torven ignored the woman as his eyes seemed to study her, moving from her face and down her body.

Trista's cheeks flushed. She wasn't used to being stared at by men, and certainly not being given such a thorough once-over. She couldn't help thinking that he must be disappointed as his eyes returned to hers.

He raised a large hand to her face, cupping her chin in his palm and stroking her cheek with his thumb. "So soft and small."

Her heart hammered in her chest so loudly she was afraid he could hear it. "Not *that* small."

The corner of his mouth twitched. "To me you are."

His eyes went to her lips, and he brushed his thumb over them. She almost moaned out loud, and her knees felt like they might buckle.

"Trista." Reina's voice jerked her back to reality.

What was she doing, letting herself get pulled under the spell of another good-looking bad boy who was nothing but trouble? Hadn't she finally escaped all that? Being taken onto the space station had been the ultimate do-over, a chance to reinvent herself and make the right choices, this time. And that did not include falling for aliens being charged with treason, no matter how hot they were.

She pushed his hand away. "I'm not your mate anymore."

Something flickered across his face and he took her hand in his, lifting it and kissing her open palm more gently than she would have expected from such a hulking guy. "You will always be mine."

She snatched her hand back as if she'd been burned at the same time one of the guards reached for Torven's arm. He spun and disarmed the man so quickly Trista barely saw it happen.

Reina gasped and dropped Trista's arm as she put both of her hands to her cheeks.

Torven turned and wrapped one arm around Trista's waist, pulling her flush to him with a single jerk. "I am sorry. I did not want things to be this way."

Before she could scream, he held the blaster to her side. The guards froze, even though their blasters were trained on him.

"I'm leaving the station, and I'm taking the Earth female with me. Unless you want the death of a tribute bride on your hands, you'll step aside."

"Let him go," Dorn said. "We can't let him kill the tribute."

Trista knew she and her fellow Earthlings were important to the Drexians, but as she watched all the blasters lower and the guards look on with tortured frustration, she understood implicitly just how valuable each human woman had to be.

Reina's usually gray skin had lost several shades of color, looking pasty as Torven backed her down the hall. Trista hoped the high-strung alien wouldn't blame herself, although her wringing hands already implied otherwise.

Even though her heart was thumping in her chest, she did not believe he would hurt her. His grip on her wasn't painful, and as he backed her down the corridor, it felt like they were almost dancing backward with her feet barely skimming the floor.

The Drexian guards followed them, but Dorn held them back and continued to instruct them to hold their fire.

"This is where we leave you," Torven said, when they reached a set of wide curved doors. "Don't follow us."

The doors slid open and he pulled her through, no longer holding her flush to him, but pulling her behind with one hand as he darted across the wide hangar bay. Mechanics and pilots moved out of the way as he sent a few sprays of blaster fire into the air.

"Everyone get back," he yelled, his voice echoing off the metal walls and floor. A station-wide alarm began wailing, and he cursed under his breath.

Torven rapidly located a black-hulled shuttle, and waved the blaster for her to go inside first. Once inside, Trista sank into one of the pilot seats and watched as he easily powered up the ship, his blaster never lowering. The interior of the ship was as dark and sleek as the outside, with a wide, shiny control panel flashing with lights.

The shuttle vibrated as the engine spun up. She'd never been on a spaceship before. Well, she'd been on one when she was brought to the station from Earth, but she'd been unconscious for that trip, so it didn't count. She'd only ever flown on an airplane once, and that hadn't gone well. She quickly scanned the cockpit. Nope, no barf bags. Damn, she hoped she didn't puke all over him.

Closing her eyes tightly, she cracked them open only when she felt him strapping her into the seat with the safety harness. His face was only inches away from hers as he quickly tugged the straps snug across her chest. He met her gaze, then dropped it as he fell into his own seat, his hands flying across the screen.

From the corner of her eye, Trista saw figures running toward them as the ship shot forward, flew across the flight deck, and rocketed through the wide mouth of the hangar bay and out into space, banking a sharp left as it flew away from the Boat.

Trista swallowed hard as Torven entered a series of commands. Then, they were pushed back into their seats, the stars transforming into streaks of light. She put a hand over her mouth to keep from being sick and to keep herself from crying. She didn't need to look back to know the station was gone, along with the only people she knew.

CHAPTER FIVE

"Are you okay?" Torven asked, giving a quick glance at the petite woman next to him. She'd opened her eyes, but her fingers still dug into the armrests of the chair.

"You kidnapped me." She sounded more shocked than frightened, which was good. Despite dragging her off the station with a blaster pointed at her, he had not wanted to terrify the female.

After looking at her image for weeks, he felt like he knew her already, and that she was a part of his life. When he'd seen her on the station, the sense of familiarity had amplified. Being close to her had unlocked all the longing and desire that had been building within him, and touching her was like being jolted by electricity. His fingers still tingled from where he'd run them over the softness of her face.

"I am sorry."

She stared at him, her pretty pink mouth hanging open. "Seriously? That's all you've got?"

He didn't reply. What could he say? He had snatched a tribute bride off the Boat while threatening to shoot her. His stomach tightened as he thought of the looks on the guards' faces. If they hadn't thought he was guilty before, they certainly did now.

His actions had not been those of an honorable Drexian warrior, much less one who belonged to Inferno Force. He squeezed his eyes shut and tried not to think about how quickly his life had unraveled. Had he made a horrible mistake by escaping the station and becoming a fugitive? A desperate fear clawed at him, and forced him to take deep breaths and concentrate on the readouts on the console.

He looked over at her again, then stood quickly and put one hand around her neck.

"What the hell?" She struggled, her eyes wild as she stared up at him.

"Hold still." He used his other hand to lift her hair and feel the back of her neck. There it was—the small scar. He knew from other Drexians that tribute brides were implanted with trackers. That would have to go if he didn't want a fleet of Drexian trackers on his tail.

Torven dropped her hair and pulled a curved blade off the wall behind him. "Don't move if you don't want to lose your head." He leaned her forward and made a tiny, razor-sharp incision over the scar, trying to ignore the sound of Trista sucking in her breath. He replaced the blade and squeezed the skin around the cut, plucking out the small chip that emerged. Dropping it to the floor, he ground it beneath his heel.

"Here." He pulled her own hand up and pressed against the wound. "Apply pressure until I bandage it."

Torven opened one of the built-in cabinets and removed the med kit, popping it open and retrieving a skin graft bandage. He pushed Trista's hand out of the way and held the square bandage to her skin, watching it meld into the flesh and stop the bleeding. "There. That should do it."

He replaced the med kit and dropped back in his chair.

A hand slapped his arm. Torven looked over to see the blonde glaring at him, her eyes glittering with tears as she felt the back of her neck. "You Drexians may think you can just snatch women from Earth whenever you like, but I'm not your property." Her voice rose an octave. "And you can't just cut things out of me like that."

"I apologize if I hurt you. I had to remove the tracker so they can't follow us. And I do not think you are my property," he said. "You are my mate."

She swiped at her eyes. "Not according to Reina and Serge. They said you were a criminal, and I was being matched to another warrior."

Torven's heat rose. "I am innocent, and you are mine."

She appeared to shrink into herself, her shoulders hunching forward. "Not unless I agree. You can't force me."

He recoiled at the word. "I would never force you. You are mine to protect."

She gave a small snort of laughter. "When have I heard that before?"

Torven studied her as she pulled her arms in tight, folding them across her chest. She was afraid of him. He'd been stupid and impulsive to bring her, and now she was terrified of him.

"I'm afraid it was necessary to bring you with me," he said, forcing himself to speak calmly. "I needed to get away before I was convicted for something I didn't do."

She cut her eyes to him. "So, you committed a crime to prove you didn't commit a crime?"

Torven opened his mouth to reply, and then closed it again. When she put it like that, his plan didn't sound so great. "I would not expect you to understand."

"What's to understand? You used me to get off the station because you knew the guards wouldn't risk hurting me, and your buddy Dorn didn't try to stop you, because he wanted you to get away." She let out a breath. "So, what's the plan? Use me as leverage until you somehow prove you're innocent? Ransom me for your freedom?"

He cocked an eyebrow at her.

Trista shrugged. "This isn't the first really bad and seriously illegal plan I've been roped into."

Torven watched her as she returned her gaze to space. Perhaps the Earth female wasn't as fragile as he'd thought, although it seemed clear she was scared of him. He couldn't help letting his eyes wander down to the soft curves of her body, especially the way the safety straps crisscrossing her chest seemed to push her breasts up. The black shirt she wore was thin and loose, but he'd noticed on the station that her pants were not. Those hugged the swell of her hips and ass, which he'd felt when he'd pressed her body against his.

Torven looked away as his cock begin to harden and gave his head a brusque shake. He could not afford distractions. Not when his life was at stake. Not even from his mate.

She's not your mate anymore, a little voice in the back of his head reminded him. *Convicts don't get tribute brides. Not that this one wants you, anyway. Not after you've terrified her.*

He grunted as he checked the readouts on the console, making sure the cloaking technology was working properly before bringing them out of light speed and laying in a course.

He would not be a convict once he proved that he was being framed. Dorn had said he would help him, and Torven trusted his Inferno Force brother with his life. He'd have to, unless he wanted to spend the rest of his life running from his own people.

"Hello?" Trista's voice pulled him from his thoughts. "Earth to Torven."

He blinked at her a few times. "You know my name."

Her cheeks colored. "They told me your name a while ago."

He noticed her looking at the flame insignia on his uniform. "Inferno Force."

She nodded. "Like Dorn."

"Like Dorn," he said.

"So, you guys are supposed to be the biggest badass Drexians, right?"

"Something like that," he said, suddenly aware that his clothes were wrinkled and dirty, as was he. He hadn't been allowed to change or bathe before reaching the station, and he knew he must look terrible.

She, on the other hand, carried the faint scent of flowers. He'd smelled it when he'd stood close to her, and if he inhaled deeply, he could smell it now. He jerked his attention back to the controls.

Focus, Torven.

"So, what's the plan?" Trista asked. "We clearly can't stay in this shuttle forever."

Torven swallowed hard. He didn't want to admit that he didn't have a plan beyond getting off the space station, but she was right. Living on the shuttle wasn't an option. Not only would it eventually be tracked, but there was a limited supply of rations.

He swiped at the console and a star chart appeared on the screen. Scanning nearby space, he located an inhabited planet. Class M. Trading colony. The perfect place to lay low for a while, because so many different ships would be coming and going, and one shuttle wouldn't be noticed. He plotted a course for the planet.

"We just need to evade the Drexians until Dorn can come up with the evidence to clear us."

"I think you mean 'you,'" Trista muttered.

"You are with me now," he said. "And you are keeping me from being blown out of the sky. My people would never risk you."

"Would you?"

He held her eyes. "I would die to protect you. You are my mate."

She looked away, her cheeks becoming a mottled patchwork of pink. "You don't even know me. How do you know you'll even want me?"

He thought of how much he did want her, and his cock stiffened. He grunted and looked away, turning his focus back to the console. "I know."

"Listen," Trista said. "I know you guys are big on honor and duty, but you don't have to do this."

"Do what? Defend myself against false accusations?"

Trista waved a hand at him. "No, you should probably do that. I mean, me. I'm sure you could request a supermodel, since you're part of Inferno Force."

"Supermodel?" He shrugged. "I do not know what this is."

She turned her gaze out the front window of the ship. "Someone really hot like you."

He knew the human culture was different from his, but he did not understand why this small, pale female thought she was not appealing. His cock throbbed just being near her, and he had to force himself to think of anything but running his hands over every soft curve of her body. Unless this was her way of getting out of being mated to him.

"Do you wish to be released from our bond?"

Her head turned quickly toward him. "That's not what I meant. I only thought you might not..."

Torven reached out one long arm and brushed his finger down the side of her cheek. "For me, there is only you. Whoever these supermodels are, I do not want them."

She sucked in a quick breath, touching her cheek where he'd stroked her.

He stood quickly and caused her to jump in her seat. "Now that we have settled that, I need to get out of this uniform."

Her eyes widened, but she didn't say anything as he walked to the back of the shuttle and opened one of the flush-panel cabinets built into the ebony walls. He found a clean pair of standard-issue black pants and a gray shirt and gratefully shrugged off his uniform jacket.

Torven glanced over to the female, who sat facing away from him. He'd have to wait until they reached the colony to bathe, but at least his clothes would be clean.

He pivoted away from her as he pulled the clean shirt over his head, then dropped his uniform pants around his ankles. Before he could step out of them, a blast of heat hit his back. His head was sluggish as he tried to turn back around. Had their ship been fired on?

Another hit made him sink to his knees, pivoting as he fell. The last thing he saw as his eyes fluttered closed was Trista standing over him, holding a blaster.

CHAPTER SIX

She couldn't believe she'd actually done it. She'd stunned her Drexian fiancé. Well, the guy who'd been her fiancé before he'd been accused of treason.

Trista looked down at where the massive alien lay facedown on the floor of the shuttle, with his pants around his ankles. "Shit, shit, shit. Now what?"

Her hands shook as she looked down at the blaster to confirm she'd set it to stun, tossed it into her seat and rubbed both hands across her forehead, feeling the beads of sweat along her hairline. What had she done?

"You freaked out and shot him," she mumbled to herself, bending down and touching her fingers to the side of his neck.

She didn't know if Drexian anatomy was the same as human, but she soon found a steady pulse. She held her fingers in place, comforted by the thrumming. At least she hadn't killed him. She let out the breath she didn't know she'd been holding, and stifled a sob.

She really hadn't meant to hurt him. She just hated to feel so powerless again, and the thought of another man dictating her life had set her off. Even if it was a guy who seemed to like her. Trista knelt down. It wasn't actually Torven's fault that she hadn't gotten over her asshole ex-boyfriend. She knew that every guy wasn't like Rick, but she'd also promised herself that she'd never be afraid of a man ever again.

It had taken every bit of strength she'd had to get away from her ex, and she'd done it all on her own. Everyone had looked the other way when he treated her like garbage. There were never any bruises—at least, not ones you could see—and he'd always waited until they were alone to unleash his worst verbal abuse. Even the other girlfriends in the bike club hadn't wanted to get involved and help her. Finally leaving him had been the hardest thing she'd ever done, and she never wanted to have to do something like that again.

She looked at the broad back of the prone Drexian, his muscular shoulders stretching the T-shirt. She hadn't actually been afraid of him. Not the way she'd been with Rick. She smiled as she realized Torven was bigger than Rick. By a lot. He could have taken her ex easily, and it made her oddly pleased to know that her new fiancé could beat up the guy who'd made her life hell.

As big as Torven was—and he had to be nearly seven feet tall—he didn't feel dangerous and mean. If she was being honest, he'd excited her. Maybe that was what actually scared her. She hadn't felt such an instant attraction to anyone before, not even to Rick. There was something in Torven's gaze that made her feel like she was under a spell, which was the last thing she wanted to feel.

When she'd originally arrived on the space station and learned about the tribute bride program, she'd been both shocked and relieved. Shocked that she'd been picked, since Rick had done a pretty good job of convincing her no one else would ever want someone like her. But mostly relieved that he'd never be able to find her again. Being taken by Torven had stirred up all that old fear, and even though her gut told her he wasn't like Rick, her fight-or-flight instinct had kicked in.

"Sorry," she whispered as she stared down at him. Her gaze drifted from the thick, swirling, black tattoos covering his biceps, down to his bare legs, and the firm ass only covered by a gunmetal-gray pair of tight-fitting boxer briefs. Damn, he was gorgeous.

She rested one hand on the expanse of his back and her fingers brushed a raised bump through the T-shirt fabric. Her breath caught in her throat. Were these the nodes she'd heard the other tribute brides talking about? She knew Drexian males had a series of bumps along their spine. She also knew these bumps hardened when they were turned on. Or was it touching them that made them aroused? It was one of the two, or maybe both.

Trista couldn't resist running her fingers down the row of nodes. From what she could tell, there was a node at every vertebrae. She stopped when she reached the waistband of his boxer briefs, her heart pounding. She knew she shouldn't go any lower. Hell, she shouldn't even be touching him now. What kind of a pervert shoots someone and then feels them up?

She snatched her hand back, her face burning. "Get it together, Trista."

Torven moaned, and she dived for the blaster, fumbling with it and knocking it from the chair to the floor. She fell back and scooped up the sleek, metallic weapon, then scrambled up and pointed it at him. He didn't move, so she relaxed. Was she really prepared to shoot him again? She didn't want to kill the guy.

But what did she want? She stood and looked out the window of the shuttle. They were still flying along the course he'd set in, which was good. She didn't relish the idea of crashing into a planet.

She glanced down at the smooth, black console with its blinking lights and illuminated star chart. Trista could fix just about anything with an engine, but computers were another matter, so none of the readouts made sense to her. Should she try to get a message back to the space station? Where were the comms anyway? Symbols covered the console, and none of them were anything close to English. The universal translator that had been implanted behind her ear when she'd been taken up to the space station allowed her to understand alien languages, but it didn't mean she could read them.

Did she really want to turn Torven in? If she did, he was as good as dead. Not only would they try him for treason, but now he was guilty of kidnapping her and evading arrest. She understood why he did it, especially if he was actually innocent like he claimed, but she doubted the bigwig Drexians would.

She stole a quick look over her shoulder. He was still lying motionless on the floor. But what if he was guilty? If he really did betray his people and conspire with the enemy, wasn't he a danger to everyone on the space station? She'd only been there a few weeks, but she already considered some of the other tribute brides to be friends. She even cared about the crazy wedding planner Serge, and the neurotic liaison Reina. The thought of any of them getting hurt made her stomach twist into a knot.

But Commander Dorn believed him, Trista reminded herself. Dorn was working to prove Torven's innocence. That had to mean something. The Drexian commander didn't strike her as someone who would be easily fooled. If Dorn was willing to go out on a limb for the fellow warrior, it meant he was already convinced.

Trista's hands hovered over the console. She couldn't turn him in. Not if there was a chance he was innocent. "As if I even know how to send out an SOS," she said to herself with a shake of her head.

A flashing red light appeared on the console, and she squinted down at it. That didn't look good. Another blinking light appeared, and then another, until the entire screen was lit up like a Christmas tree. She didn't know what it meant, but she guessed it was nothing good.

She bent over Torven. She needed to get him up before they flew into something or blew up. Hopefully he wouldn't be too angry that she'd shot him. Grabbing his far arm, Trista heaved him over onto his back, breathing heavily from the effort.

"Torven." She shook him gently and tried to keep her voice calm. "Torven. I need you to get up."

Nothing. She put a finger under his nose. He was breathing. That was good.

She shook him harder. "Tor—"

Before she could get his name out, his eyes flew open and he'd grabbed her and flipped her onto her back. The air went out of her, as his body pressed against hers. He grabbed her wrists and pulled her arms over her head, pinning them to the floor behind her and holding them there with one hand. His legs were between hers and something big and hard pressed into her stomach. She tried to regain her breath, even as she knew it would be pointless to struggle.

Her body responded instantly to having his pressed against it. Her nipples hardened, and without thinking, she arched her back so that they brushed his chest. A small gasp escaped her lips, only inches from his face.

His pupils widened, making his gold eyes darker, as they flashed both anger and confusion. He panted as he looked down at her, tightening his grip on her wrists. "You shot me."

CHAPTER SEVEN

Torven felt her quiver beneath him. He didn't mean to scare her, but he couldn't let her go, either. Not after she'd shot him with his own blaster. Twice.

If he was being honest, he also liked the feel of her soft body underneath his. The hard points of her nipples brushed his chest every time she breathed in, and he fought the urge to bend down and nip at them through her thin shirt.

"You tried to kill me," he said, attempting to ignore the distraction of his throbbing cock and rapid heart rate.

"I didn't want to kill you." Her voice shook as she spoke. "I set the blaster on its lowest setting before I fired. It was supposed to stun you."

He grunted and saw that tears were filling her eyes. "Why?"

She strained against his hands. "Oh, I don't know. You'd just kidnapped me and cut me open."

He studied her face—the flush of pink on her cheeks, the long, brown lashes framing wide eyes, the lower lip that was plumper than the top. A single tear slipped out from under one eyelid, and his irritation melted away. "I am sorry if I frightened you."

She opened her eyes and glared at him. "You don't scare me, but I don't like being told what to do."

He saw that her pupils were dilated, making her blue eyes look much darker, and he watched her tongue moisten her bottom lip. He loosened his grip on her wrists and lowered one hand to her face, wiping away the tear streak with his thumb. "I would never hurt you."

Trista took a halting breath. "You have an odd way of showing that, considering you held me at gunpoint and dragged me off the station."

"I explained that it was the only way to get away. If I didn't escape, they would have convicted me on false evidence." He took a breath. "They would have taken you from me. I couldn't bear that."

She shook her head. "You keep saying things like that, but you don't know me."

"That's where you're wrong." He dragged his thumb across her lower lip, feeling a desperate need to taste her. She was his mate, the human female he'd been matched with, and who he'd been on his way to marry. He'd been staring at her image for weeks, but the reality of her was even better than what he'd imagined. He loved her small body, her soft curves, and her pale hair. She was his, body and soul, and Torven knew she'd been his from the moment he first saw her in the corridor of the space station. "I know we're meant to be together."

"How can you know something like that? I don't know you at all," she said, her voice breathy. "The only thing I know is your name, and that you're a warrior with Inferno Force."

Her chest rose and fell underneath his, the swell of her breasts a sharp contrast to the hard planes of his muscles. He hesitated, even as the blood pounded in his ears. According to the Drexian High Command, she was no longer his mate. He'd lost her the second he was charged with treason. There was no doubt he'd have been found guilty courtesy of the trumped-up charges, and Trista would have been reassigned to a warrior they considered more worthy. It didn't matter that he got a jolt every time he looked at her or that her body responded to his the way it did. She was no longer his to claim, even though the desire to make her his was almost overpowering.

"I am a Drexian warrior sworn to protect my people and others in the galaxy who cannot defend themselves." He released his hold on her wrists, but she did not move her arms. "And I will protect you with my life no matter how many times you shoot me."

She met his eyes and her lips twitched up. "That might be the nicest and strangest thing any man has ever said to me."

He was very aware that his cock was still hard and still pressed against her. Claiming her now when she was no longer his tribute bride would be dishonorable, he reminded himself. Until he was proven innocent, he could not take what was no longer his. No matter how he felt or how she made him feel, he knew that even touching her like he was doing now would not be looked upon favorably. Even despite knowing in his gut that she was meant to be his mate. Torven bowed his head, breathing in the floral scent of her hair as he tried to regain control and not scream in frustration.

An alarm sounding from the pilot's console finally made him lift his head.

"That's why I was trying to wake you," she said. "Something's wrong with the shuttle, but I don't know what."

He jumped up, pulling her along with him and tugging his pants up around his waist. Spotting the blaster on the floor, he picked it up and hooked it on the belt of his uniform, casting her a look and watching her blush in response. "I trust you will not shoot me again?"

Trista held up both palms. "I promise. Shooting you means shooting the only pilot on board."

"I hope to one day give you a few more reasons not to shoot me." He motioned for her to sit as he scanned the blinking lights. "Until then, you may want to strap in."

“Strap in?” She fumbled with the straps. “Are we going to crash?”

“Not if I can help it,” he said, as he peered at the warnings flashing across the screen, “but it looks like we got hit with a solar flare. One engine is disabled, and the other is damaged.”

Trista looked over at him, concern etched on her face. “How many engines do we have?”

He fastened his own safety straps. “Two.”

She clutched both armrests. “What’s the worst-case scenario?”

He raised an eyebrow at her. “You want to know the worst thing that could happen?”

She bobbed her head up and down. “I like to know the worst case. That way, I’m not surprised when bad things happen.”

“I’m not going to let the worst case happen.” He swiped his fingers across the console, checking the system readouts and trying to keep the panic out of his voice as the ship shook and jerked. No way was he going to give her the worst-case scenario, since it was difficult to determine which of the possible outcomes would be worse than the other. Floating in space while life support slowly dwindled? Crashing into an uninhabitable planet? Exploding into a thousand pieces?

Torven made a quick decision and changed course. The shuttle was too damaged to continue to fly safely, and he couldn’t fix it without landing it first. They’d have to set down at the nearest class M planet, even if it wasn’t one he’d heard of.

He leaned in closer to the star chart. The nearest habitable planet didn’t even have a name, just a letter and series of numbers —C-459. That wasn’t a good sign. That meant it hadn’t been colonized, so there were no outposts, no bases, no inhabitants. Of course, since he was a fugitive, this was also a good thing. No inhabitants meant no one who could turn him in for the bounty that was no doubt on his head.

“We need to land,” he said, glancing over at Trista. He noticed she was pressing her lips together tightly. “Are you okay?”

She waved a hand in his direction and nodded, her skin a pale shade of green. "I haven't flown a lot, and this isn't the smoothest ride."

The shuttle pitched to one side, and he tried to right it as Trista clamped a hand over her mouth. The planet came into closer view, and Torven swallowed hard. He hoped the solid-white orb was covered in a thick cloud cover and was not just a ball of ice, although his malfunctioning sensors gave him temperature readings that made his stomach clench. He rapped his knuckles on the console and the numbers flickered. He hoped they were wrong.

Gripping the edge of the console for balance, he adjusted their settings and attempted to keep the shuttle steady as they approached the atmosphere. The hull rattled and groaned. Trista's eyes were closed, but she wasn't holding a hand over her mouth, so Torven decided to take that as a good sign.

They dipped below the thick layer of clouds, dropping rapidly as the remaining engine spluttered. Torven fought to keep the nose of the ship up and slow their descent, but the ship fought against him. He stole another glance at Trista, her cheeks pale and her mouth moving as she silently repeated something over and over. Even in her current state of panic, he found her fascinating, and he forced himself to pull his gaze from staring at her pretty lips and imagining all the things she could do with them.

Torven turned back to the viewscreen with determination. He would not let them crash. As they exited the clouds, he got his first look at the planet's terrain, and had to stop himself from uttering a Drexian curse. Now he understood why the planet had no colonies or outposts.

The surface was covered with ice and snow as far as he could see. Geysers of steam shot high into the air from cracks in the frozen ground, and the moisture froze in the air and cascaded back down as pellets of ice. Wide valleys of white were broken up by tall, craggy mountains, which he knew he'd need to avoid. He swiveled his head to see if there was any place on the surface that wasn't frozen, but everything was white.

Torven pressed his lips together, glad Trista wasn't watching. He flew the shuttle over a sharp mountain range and spotted what he hoped was a viable landing spot below. Angling the ship lower, he braced himself as they touched down, then attempted to hold the nose up so they wouldn't cartwheel from the momentum. The ship jolted from the impact, and Trista yelped as they hit down a few more times, skidding into thick snow and crunching through ice and finally slowing to a stop.

Torven released his grip and the breath he'd been holding. They were alive, and the ship was in one piece. He turned to Trista, who stared out the front of the ship where ice covered half of the nose.

"You owe me big time, buddy," she said. "I hate cold weather."

CHAPTER EIGHT

"You've got to be kidding me," Trista mumbled, as she stared out the front of the ship.

"Kidding you?" Torven tilted his head. "You think I am trying to make you laugh?"

Trista waved a hand. "Nothing. Never mind. I can't believe we're marooned on a planet covered with nothing but ice."

Torven glanced down at the console. "It is not ideal."

"Not ideal?" Trista gaped at him. "Ya think?"

"It was this, or lose power and float in space."

"No," Trista said, her voice louder. "I could still be on the station having lunch with my nervous liaison Reina and talking to nutty Serge about the wedding, although I guess we wouldn't have been talking about the wedding since there wasn't going to be one. But at least I'd be there, and I'd be safe. Now I'm stranded God knows where with a guy I don't even know, who's on the run from his own people because they think he's a traitor."

Torven was silent for a moment. "I am sorry you are missing lunch."

"Seriously?" She swung her head to face him. "That's what you got out of all of that?"

"If you want me to be sorry for taking you off the station, I am not."

Trista's irritation flared. Of course, he wasn't sorry. The only way he got away was by threatening her safety. Being stranded on an uninhabited planet was better than being convicted of treason, so he was coming out ahead no matter what. "Typical."

"What is typical?"

"Typical alpha male who always gets what he wants," Trista said, hearing the anger in her voice. "Funny that it never works out well for me."

"You think this is what I wanted?" Torven's voice rose and he stood from his chair. "I was on my way to the station to meet my mate when I was told that not only was she to be taken from me, but that I was being accused of something I did not do. Something I would never do. I arrived on the station as an accused traitor instead of a warrior and a groom."

When he stood, he towered over her, and she was even more aware of just how huge he was. The massive bulge in his pants was now at eye level, and Trista quickly looked away, her mouth going dry.

He leaned over her, putting one hand on either side of her. "I should be naked on a huge bed in some holographic suite with you underneath me and your pretty little legs wrapped around me as you beg me for more. But instead, I'm running for my life and trying to keep you alive in the process. So, this is far from what I wanted either, mate."

She tried to swallow as she looked up at him and into his black-lined eyes. He was so close she could feel his breath mingling with her own.

"You're pretty sure of yourself," she managed to say. "You're assuming I'd fall into bed with you."

"Not assuming." He lowered his head so his lips brushed her ear. "Making an educated guess."

His words sent a spasm down her spine and she shivered. She

hated that the briefest touch from him made her body feel like it was on fire. More evidence that she was still attracted to the wrong kind of men.

He traced a finger down her neck to the hollow of her throat. "When we get out of here and I'm proven innocent, you will be my mate and you will beg me to take you again and again."

Trista shook her head but was unable to speak. Her heart pounded and her skin flushed where he'd touched her. "That's a lot of 'ifs.'"

He straightened, his face convulsing with an emotion she couldn't place. "Yes, it is."

She was relieved to have space between them so she could catch her breath. Torven held her gaze for a moment before turning and heading to the back of the ship.

Even though she was breathing heavily, and a trickle of sweat slid down the back of her neck—courtesy of Torven getting her all hot and bothered—she rubbed her arms for warmth. Just looking outside and seeing nothing but ice and snow made her shiver and miss the heat emanating from the big Drexian.

"So, what's the plan now?" Trista asked, unhooking herself from the chair and following Torven to the back of the shuttle. She may still be pissed at him, but she also knew they'd need to work together to get out of their current situation.

"Assess our supplies. Fix the ship. Leave before we're discovered." His words were clipped, and she could tell he was worried and perhaps not totally confident they could accomplish all those things.

She smelled something burning and suspected it was one of their engines. That wouldn't be an easy fix. One by-product of dating losers who were more interested in their cars and motorcycles than in her was that she'd gotten to know her way around engines. If she wanted to spend time with them, she'd had to hang out in the garage and learn which tool did what. Over the years, she'd discovered a talent for mechanics and, even now, the possibility of getting her hands on a spaceship engine excited her.

Trista swiveled her head to take in the dark interior of the shuttle. "What supplies? Extra engine components?"

Torven pressed a panel on one wall and it popped up, revealing hidden shelves stacked with everything from metal canisters of water to blankets to shiny, sealed packets that looked remarkably like MREs. She picked up one of the packets and, even though she couldn't read the Drexian words printed on the front; she saw through the clear-plastic window that it was some sort of snack food. She pulled back the seal to open it and popped one of the crispy chips in her mouth.

"You like padwump rind?" Torven asked as he watched her chew, his expression bemused.

Trista swallowed the salty mouthful. "What's padwump rind?"

"Padwump is a type of creature." Torven motioned to the packet. "And that is fried bits of its skin."

Trista froze, looking at the chips and seeing a fleshy texture she hadn't noticed before. "Fried skin?"

Torven smiled widely now. "You've adapted better to our ways than I imagined."

Trista thought about the fried skin she'd just swallowed and put a hand to her stomach. So much for Drexian snack food. She reached for one of the metal canisters. "This is water, right?"

He nodded as he watched her chug half the contents in an attempt to rid her mouth of the salty and savory flavor of deep-fried animal skin. "We should probably be a little more careful with our food and water intake since we don't know how long we'll be here."

Trista looked down at the bottle she'd nearly drained. "Sorry."

"It is fine. Like you said, you missed lunch."

She gave a small snort of laughter and placed the water canister back on the shelf. "It looks like we have food and water for at least a few days."

"All shuttles are stocked with rations and water for a week, but we should still be careful."

"You think we'll be here for more than a week?" Trista asked.

"I hope not, but even if we get this shuttle flying again, we can't guarantee we'll find a place to restock supplies. We won't be able to fly into just any outpost."

She eyed him. "Because they'll be looking for you?"

He nodded without looking at her. "Drexians excel at hunting, and I have no doubt the High Command will send out their best."

Her stomach tightened at the thought of being hunted. As annoyed as she was with Torven, she didn't like the idea of him being the prey.

He ran his hands along the shelves as if he was looking for something in particular, then he produced a shimmery pile of fabric. "Just what I was hoping to find."

"What is that?" she asked as he unfurled the fabric. "It looks like a jumpsuit."

Torven stepped into the legs and the fabric pulled taut across his muscular legs. "It is an environmental suit designed to protect the wearer from any hazardous conditions."

Trista watched him tug it over his torso and then up over his broad shoulders. She touched the sleek fabric on his bicep. "Is it insulated? It looks like a fancy version of Spandex."

He furrowed his brow. "Does Spandex adapt to its surroundings and change color so the wearer appears invisible?"

Her mouth fell open as he snapped a band around his wrist and touched it, causing the fabric to become as black and glossy as the walls of the shuttle. She could still see the outlines of his body, but only because she stood inches away from him. Otherwise, he appeared to be a floating head. "So, when you go out there…?"

"I will blend with the background and be protected from the freezing temperatures."

"Do you have one of those for me?" she asked.

"You should stay in here where it's safe. Take inventory of our supplies while I assess the damage to the ship and attempt to repair it."

Trista folded her arms across her chest, feeling her irritation return. "I appreciate the caveman gesture, but you need me out there."

He pressed his eyes together. "I need you in here."

Trista hesitated, wondering whether she should tell him about her mechanical skills. No one on the station knew about this decidedly unfeminine side of her, mostly because she didn't want to explain how she'd acquired the skill. There had never been an appropriate time to casually mention she'd dated members of a criminal biker gang. But now she was stranded on a floating ball of ice with a ship that needed fixing. If there was ever a time to tell someone, this was it. Anyway, who was Torven going to tell? He was an outlaw who might end up in prison, and the planet they'd landed on didn't look like it had life. On top of that, her gut told her he wouldn't be the type to share her secrets, anyway.

"I can smell the burning engine from inside. Now, I may not be an expert in spaceships, but an engine is an engine. I've helped rebuild everything from classic Camaros to vintage Harleys. You need me out there."

He gaped at her for a moment. "You were a mechanic? They did not mention that on your information."

"That's because no one here knows that all my ex-boyfriends were grease monkeys, and that I learned by helping them." She shrugged. "It's not the kind of information you share with girls who are ballerinas and socialites."

"Grease monkeys?"

She grinned at his confused expression. "It means they worked on cars and bikes."

He frowned. "How many ex-boyfriends?"

"It doesn't matter," she said, wanting to change the subject. "They were all assholes, and now I never have to see them again."

Torven stared at her for a moment, then produced another suit from the shelf. He cut his eyes to her slip-on shoes and pulled down a pair of boots. “You are intriguing, Trista from Iowa.”

She pulled on the suit, the fabric sagging around her much smaller limbs, and slipped on the too-big boots. “You are officially the first person to ever think I’m intriguing.”

He clamped a band around her wrist and pressed a button and her suit constricted around her body and morphed to black. “You only need one.”

Her wrist was warm where he touched her, and she looked up into his eyes. It was one thing to resist a bossy alpha male; it was another thing to resist a guy who looked at her like he did. Her entire body seemed to tingle at his touch, as if she were being awakened.

Trista glanced away and focused on the mission. Fix the ship, get off the planet, and do not fall under the spell of the big Drexian.

She gulped as her pulse fluttered. Easier said than done.

CHAPTER NINE

Torven watched as Trista ran her fingers over the wiring surrounding the shuttle's engine. They stood at the back of the ship, with a wide, metal panel open, exposing the guts of the vessel.

"We got lucky," Trista said, her voice muffled by the hood covering her head and the transparent window over her face. "The cold actually stopped the engine from burning up."

Torven gazed at the wide valley around them and the sheet of ice that was the ground. He wasn't sure if lucky was the word he'd use to describe their current situation. Aside from them, there was no sign of life. He couldn't imagine how anything could live in such a frozen, barren place.

Despite the frigid temperatures outside, he didn't feel cold. He glanced down at the environmental suit keeping him warm, the fabric now white against the snowy terrain. Apart from Trista's face earnestly studying the damaged engine, the rest of her body faded into the background, and he knew his did the same.

He watched her work, feeling a strange rush of warmth when he saw how animated her face became as she inspected the mass of wires and metal. He'd never expected an Earth female to have a talent for mechanics, although, if he was being honest, he hadn't bothered to learn much about human women. Aside from her photo and her name, Torven had created the rest of his image of her entirely in his own head. Boy, had he been wrong.

He didn't know if all Earth women were similar, but this was no placid creature hanging on his every word. Trista was nothing like the alien females he'd encountered on the pleasure planets. It was foolish that he'd thought she would be. Serving on Inferno Force had taught him a lot of things, but how to handle a human woman had not been one of them.

He knew she desired him. At least, her body reacted to his. He also knew that wasn't enough. He'd seen the resistance in her eyes, and knew she'd been hurt before. The thought of the ex-boyfriends she mentioned causing her pain made his blood boil. He didn't understand how a male with any honor could ever mistreat a female, but it explained why she didn't trust him. He'd have to work hard to win her over.

As soon as I've been proven innocent, he reminded himself. *As soon as she is mine again I will convince her we are meant to be together.*

Trista thumped the side of the ship. "I think if we fix these wires, we can get her up and running again."

Her voice echoed in the stillness, the hills surrounding the valley sending her words back to her. Torven didn't know when he'd experienced such complete quiet. There was no sound of birds or insects or even wind, and the silence unnerved him. He was used to the constant hum of a battleship, the loud voices of his crewmates, the raucous laughter of the mess hall. Here, there was nothing, and he didn't like it.

"Torven?" she said. "Earth to Torven."

"What do you need?" he asked, pulling his eyes back to her.

"A wire stripper and pliers, to start."

Her eyes shone with excitement, and he couldn't help but smile back. Her enthusiasm was contagious, and it pleased him to see her so happy. It was an improvement over her eyeing him suspiciously. And it really beat her shooting him.

"I will get them for you, if you will be okay out here by yourself."

She swiveled her head to take in the stretch of ice and snow. "I'm pretty sure we're the only things out here that aren't frozen solid."

He nodded and walked back to the front of the ship, his boots crunching on the packed snow and ice. He activated the entry ramp and ran up it so as not to let too much of the icy air into the shuttle. Closing it behind him, he pressed another flat panel and searched the shelf behind it for the right tools.

As his hand closed around the shiny set of pliers, the floor rumbled faintly under his feet. Was it the ship? He knew they were still running life support, but that shouldn't cause shaking. He paused, but didn't feel or hear anything else. Maybe he'd imagined it, or maybe Trista had gotten the damaged engine fired up again and that had caused the rumbling.

Torven exited the ship, closing the ramp behind him. He rejoined Trista and handed her the tools.

She smiled up at him. "Thanks."

The ground trembled again, and he put a hand on the hull to brace himself. Trista stumbled against him, dropping the pliers in the snow. He caught her and wrapped an arm around her waist to steady her.

"What was that?" she asked, not pushing away from him.

"I'm not sure." Torven pivoted as he held her, but didn't see anything in the vicinity or on the horizon.

"Maybe this planet has seismic activity, although I've never heard of a frozen volcano."

Torven remembered the geysers he'd spotted on their descent. The planet was not completely dormant, that was obvious, although he didn't see any nearby cracks in the ground or water shooting skyward.

"We should hurry," he said, more than a little concerned. "The sooner we get out of here, the better."

She stepped away from him and scooped her tool off the ground. "Agreed."

Torven rested one hand on the blaster hooked to his belt as he scanned the open space. He couldn't see anything, but his instincts told him they were not alone. As desolate as the planet seemed, he was almost certain the planet wasn't void of life. Geysers meant that there was heat beneath the surface, as well as water, and those two things usually indicated some sort of life, even if it was microscopic. The only problem was he didn't know what kind of life, how big it was, and whether it was friend or foe.

The ground trembled again, followed by a loud snap, and Torven watched open-mouthed as a crack split the ice. The thick sheet beneath them rose as if pushed up from below, and he caught Trista before she slipped under the ship as it skidded backward. Planting his feet into the snow, he held both of them in place.

"Is this an Earthquake?" Trista screamed.

Before he could answer, a large, scaly creature emerged from the crack, dripping water from its elongated white head, which it swung in their direction.

"I don't think this is a valley," Torven said, glancing at their feet. "I think we're on a frozen lake."

Trista inhaled sharply. "That explains the giant albino alligator."

Torven didn't know what alligators were, but he knew whatever this beast was, it wasn't friendly. He drew his blaster, letting go of Trista and trying to decide where on the ugly creature to fire first.

"We have to get back inside," he said, but then realized he was talking to empty air as Trista had ducked under one wing of the ship and started running in the opposite direction.

The creature locked his attention on her and gave chase, racing across the ice faster than Torven would have expected, with his short legs and flat webbed feet. Fear shot through Torven as he watched his mate being chased by a creature with enormous teeth and a thick tail that swung behind him as he ran. No way would she come out on the winning end if it caught her.

"*Grek,*" he muttered as he tore after them both, firing at the creature. His heart pounded in his ribcage as his feet thundered across the ice, and he tried to keep his arms steady and aim his blaster. Even though he hit it, the creature barely slowed. Torven guessed that its scales were protecting it from most of the damage. He kept firing, going for the legs, until he hit one and the creature started to limp. It swung around, its red eyes focusing on Torven. It roared once, the sound splitting the air, before it slipped into another crack in the ice and vanished into the water.

"Trista," he called out as he stopped and bent over at the waist to suck in air. He couldn't make out anything but a flash of movement, as her environmental suit made her blend in completely with the background.

She stopped and turned, and he could finally see her face through the clear window in the hood. Seeing that the creature was gone, she smiled and gave him a thumbs-up. A wave of relief washed over him, and his breathing began to return to normal as she started walking back toward him.

That was when another crack opened in the ground where she stood, and the gaping ice swallowed her whole.

CHAPTER
TEN

She expected to feel the frigid water as she plunged beneath the ice, but Trista's suit shielded her from the cold. She did feel the pressure of the water engulf her as she fell, and she instinctively sucked in a breath before her head went under. What she didn't expect was the pitch-blackness that instantly surrounded her. The ice was so thick light didn't penetrate beyond the crack in the surface, and she quickly sank into the dark depths.

Trista tried not to panic. There was air in her facemask, although she didn't know how long that would last. She kicked up, but it didn't feel like the motion propelled her. Her boots were too heavy and, to keep them on her feet, she'd tied the laces tightly around her ankles. Not only that, she couldn't tell which way was up and which was down anymore. It was too dark. For all she knew, she could be pushing herself deeper. She stopped and closed her eyes, willing herself not to panic.

Was this really how she was going to die? Under the frozen surface of an ice planet, after being taken from Earth and then kidnapped from the aliens who'd taken her in the first place? The whole thing seemed so ridiculous. If she didn't feel like crying, she'd want to laugh.

She took shallow breaths to conserve oxygen as something large brushed against her leg. Well, this just got better and better. Being eaten alive by that albino super-gator was definitely worse than drowning. She resisted the impulse to thrash as her lungs burned. Pointing her arms overhead and kicking up, Trista hoped she was moving in the right direction. She tilted her head back and searched for a sliver of light.

As her ears started to ring, something grasped her hand. For a moment, she thought the creature had gotten her and she jerked back. But the larger hand around hers held tight, pulling her up until they both breached the surface.

Torven hooked an arm around her waist as they bobbed in the water, holding her tightly as he gripped the edge of the ice with his other hand.

She trembled in his arms, allowing herself to sag against him.

"We need to get out," he said, pushing her up and onto the ice.

Trista's arms shook as she scrambled onto all fours and then turned to help Torven, but he was already heaving himself out. Water streamed off his suit and puddled around them both.

"You saved me," she said.

"I will always save you."

She didn't know how to respond to that. She'd never had anyone sacrifice themselves for her. Not her parents. Not her ex-boyfriends. Nobody. If there was one thing that had been impressed upon Trista over her lifetime, it was that no one would be riding in to save the day. Until now.

Torven pulled her up and looped an arm around her waist. "We need to get back to the ship."

"I'm sorry I ran," she said, feeling like she needed to apologize. If she hadn't taken off, the creature wouldn't have chased her and she wouldn't have ended up in the water. "I guess I freaked out when I saw that thing."

"Let's hope we do not see it again."

"I'll second that." Even though her legs did not feel shaky anymore, she liked the feel of Torven's strong arm around her.

They approached the ship, the sleek black hull stark against the blinding white terrain. The panel exposing the engines was still open, and the tools lay in the snow where she'd dropped them. She didn't need much longer to patch things up, and her fingers twitched at the thought of getting back to the broken machine.

"Let's go inside, first," Torven said, lowering the entry ramp by touching his wristband.

"But I'm almost done," Trista said, jerking a thumb back toward the engine.

"You almost drowned. I want to run a quick scan and make sure you're all right." He touched a hand to her suit, the droplets of water frozen into shards that fell to the ground. "At least you're not soaked."

She begrudgingly agreed, even though she felt fine. Trista reminded herself she was fine because he'd jumped in the freezing water to save her. And because the fabric of their suits kept the water from freezing them to death. The least she could do would be to let him run his scans and ease his mind.

Closing the ramp after them, he flipped back his hood before pulling a med kit out of one of the hidden cabinets and popping it open.

"They really stock these shuttles with everything, don't they?" Trista glanced around the polished, black walls and wondered what else was tucked away inside them. She stood still as he rummaged through the cabinets, the water from her soaking boots puddling at her feet. The next thing on her agenda after getting scanned? Dry boots.

Torven found the scanner he needed—a small, metallic disc—and he switched it on before turning his attention to her. "I need you to take off your suit, or at least slip it down to your waist."

She shimmied out of the environmental suit, noticing that the fabric had taken on the color of its surroundings again, and was jet-black now, instead of the white it had been outside. Since most of the ice had fallen off it outside the ship, it was also dry again. "Drexians have pretty cool technology."

Torven raised one of his eyebrows as he ran the blinking scanner down her body. "You do not have this on Earth?"

"Only on TV," she said. "The Sci-Fi channel mostly. And even there we don't have clothes that change color."

"Your planet has not achieved light-speed technology, so it makes sense that you do not have the innovations we do." He glanced at the scanner and seemed satisfied. "That is why we protect you."

"Doesn't it bother you that no one on Earth knows what you guys are doing?" she asked. "I mean, aside from a few government people."

Torven cocked his head at her. "Why would it bother me?"

"I don't know," she mumbled. "You're at war for a bunch of people who don't know you exist. They can never thank you."

"I don't defend Earth for the thanks."

"Right." Heat rushed to her cheeks. "You do it because you get a woman in return."

He shook his head. "I would do it even if I was never matched with a tribute bride. I do it because defending those weaker than us is the right thing to do."

"Hot and honorable," Trista said with a shake of her head. "I think you guys are missing a golden opportunity. If women on Earth knew about you, they'd be killing each other to volunteer as brides."

Torven put the scanner back in the med kit and snapped it shut. He pulled her environmental suit up and began zipping it closed. He paused when he reached her neck. "And you? Would you have killed to be a tribute bride?"

She laughed, but it was nervous laughter. "I doubt I'd make the cut if you had your pick of women from Earth."

"I would always pick you." He was not laughing as his eyes locked with hers.

Trista's knees wobbled, and at first, she thought it was his proximity that made her feel like the ground was shifting. She put a hand on his chest to keep from falling, and realized it wasn't just that he made her legs feel like jelly. The ship was moving.

Torven grabbed her as a loud crack sounded, and the ship listed to one side. His shoulder hit the wall of the shuttle, but he kept her from impacting.

"The ice," she said. "It must be breaking up even more."

Without speaking, he opened a cabinet and retrieved a pair of backpacks that appeared to be made out of the same fabric as the suits. He thrust one at her. "Fill it."

He opened more hidden cabinets and started jamming rations, canisters of water, and blankets into the large bags. Trista followed his lead, stuffing as much into her bag as she could, her stomach churning all the while. Did this mean they were leaving the ship and not returning? That couldn't be good. She did not want to live out her life on a planet with mutant alligators.

Torven hurried to the ship's console, his fingers flying across the shiny display. The ice cracked and groaned. The ship dropped a few feet, the nose tilting down as it slipped slowly toward a crevice and the dark water below.

Torven dashed back and grabbed her hand. "We have to go. Now."

Trista sealed the hood of her suit and hoisted her full pack onto one shoulder. She glanced at the front window of the ship as the ramp lowered, her heart racing as the yawning black mouth grew larger as the ship slid forward.

"Jump," Torven yelled, as he yanked her by the hand, and the two of them leapt off the only partially lowered ramp.

The ship fell away as her feet left the floor, and moments later she landed on the ice. Her teeth rattled in her head from the impact, but she didn't have time to shake it off before Torven had yanked her to her feet and they were running across the icy surface as it cracked beneath their feet.

Stealing a glance over her shoulder as they ran, Trista's heart sank. Their shuttle—and their only way off the ice planet—splashed into the dark waters beneath the surface, gurgling as it disappeared entirely.

They were officially stranded.

CHAPTER ELEVEN

Torven stopped once they'd reached the edge of the frozen lake. He didn't want to look back, because he knew their shuttle was gone. Seeing the empty ice would only slam the reality home, and the reality was they had no way off planet C-459.

The ground trembled under his feet, and a geyser of steam shot up a short distance away, sending tiny pellets of ice down around their heads as the steam froze in mid-air and fell back to the Earth. Not only did creatures dwell under the surface, there appeared to be a significant amount of seismic activity. So much for the planet being an uninhabited, frigid wasteland.

He looked down at Trista and at the fear in her eyes, and his stomach twisted. This was his fault. He'd brought her here, landing them on a frozen lake and marooning them on a frozen planet with seemingly no inhabitants but monstrous ones.

Peering up into the sky, he saw the single sun—a tiny glowing dot in the distance—dipping low on the horizon. He took a deep breath and resumed walking. "We need to keep moving."

Trista pulled back on his hand. "Why? Where are we going?"

Torven turned to her, not meeting her eyes. He gestured to the craggy rocks in the distance. “The best chance for shelter is in those mountains.”

Her jaw dropped. “We’re never going to reach them before dark.”

“Not if we don’t move.” He tugged her forward again.

They plodded through the snowbanks surrounding the frozen lake, and across a wide stretch of hard-packed ice, Torven never taking his eyes off the white range of mountains. Trista stumbled and he caught her by the elbow, but she sank again.

“I’m so dizzy,” she said, her voice thin.

He raised her wrist and looked at the band linked to her suit. The pure oxygen that flowed into the facemask was almost gone. Initial scans of the planet’s atmosphere had reported breathable air, but with much lower levels of oxygen than humans were used to. He knew he’d be fine, since Drexians had a greater lung capacity, but he worried about the small female. He removed his hood and inhaled the icy air.

“This is going to be cold,” he said as he lowered her hood. “Take slow breaths.”

She shivered as the air hit her face, but started breathing evenly. “That’s better. Freezing, but better.”

Scooping her up into his arms, Torven continued walking.

She slapped weakly at his chest. “Hey, He-Man. I can walk.”

He shook his head. “You’re weak. Your body is probably having a delayed reaction to going under the water.”

“You went under, too,” she said, her head resting against him. “Why aren’t you having a reaction?”

“I’m Drexian. Our training to be warriors helps us adjust to intense situations.”

She didn’t respond to that, just nodded as her eyes fluttered closed. He saw her chest rise and fall, and felt the warmth of her breath as she breathed in and out.

It was better if she slept, since Torven had a long walk to reach the mountains. His mind whirled as he trudged through the snow.

What if he couldn't find shelter before dark? Could he keep her warm enough? Could he fight off any creatures that might emerge in the night?

His worry spurred him to walk faster, the crunching of his heavy boots the only sound he could hear. After a lifetime spent doing what was right, Torven had made a series of bad decisions that had brought him to where he was. He squinted at the hard, cold ground that seemed to stretch out endlessly in front of him. Unfortunately, he'd dragged an innocent female along with him, and now her life was in danger.

"I will not let anything harm you," he promised, whispering the words out loud, even though he knew she was asleep.

He tightened his hold on Trista, pulling her closer to his chest and feeling a pang of regret. He had to keep her safe, no matter what. Not only was she his mate—at least, she had been—but he wanted to learn more about her. He was already fascinated that she knew her way around an engine, and he'd loved watching her face light up as she worked. It was clear there was more to the pale-haired creature than he'd first thought. It was also obvious that she was keeping parts of herself hidden.

He looked down at the long lashes fanned out beneath her closed eyes and the pale dots scattered across her nose. Warmth spread through his chest. More than claiming her as his, he wanted to know her. Know her as well as he knew his closest friends.

His mind went to Dakar. When Torven had been dragged out of the outpost bar, his best friend had vowed to clear his name. He wondered if the warrior had been able to discover anything that could clear him. Dakar was known for his tenacity, as well as for his ability to sweet-talk just about anyone. If there was a Drexian warrior alive who could uncover the truth behind the false charges, it was Dak.

"I'm counting on you, Dak," he said only to himself.

The thought of being proven innocent made the trek seem less daunting. He lifted his knees higher, even as his back ached and his shoulders screamed in pain. Torven could survive anything, as long as he had his honor. His eyes drifted to Trista again. Perhaps now he required one other thing.

As the sun eased lower, and slats of golden light lit up the ground in front of him, Torven began to run. He was determined to keep her safe until they were rescued. Holding her tight to his chest so she wouldn't be jostled, his legs pumped furiously.

When he reached the edge of the craggy cliffs, he stopped to breathe. His heart hammered in his chest. It had been a long time since he'd run so far, carrying so much weight. Even when he used the training simulators in the battleship's gym, he didn't have two full packs of supplies and a human.

"I like to hear a man breathing heavy," Trista mumbled, her eyes barely opening, and her words slurred.

Torven wasn't sure he'd heard her correctly. He shifted her in his arms.

"You're so big," she said, rubbing one hand across the muscles of his chest. "Just the way I like it."

He knew he'd heard that. He stared down at her. Her eyes were half open, and she looked dazed as she looked up at him. His cock twitched, as she continued to rub him.

The thinner air must be making her feel giddy, he thought, telling himself not to get aroused. The female was clearly out of it, and not thinking straight.

She nuzzled her head into his neck, and he bit back a groan. His cock strained against the tight environmental suit, despite his best efforts to convince himself this was not the time. He still needed to find shelter.

Staggering forward, Torven started to wind his way into the mountain range. Luckily, Trista appeared to have drifted off again, and he could focus on keeping them from slipping off the narrow rock ledge, instead of freeing his throbbing cock.

Darkness fell, as he spotted the low opening of a cave. The ceiling was not high enough for him to walk inside without bending over, but it extended far back, with tunnels shooting off the main cavern that led even deeper. He lowered Trista to the floor and slumped down next to her.

They'd made it. He'd found shelter for them for the night. He stretched out on the ground, his chest heaving as he tried to slow his breath. His arms and legs burned, the muscles twitching in relief that they were no longer moving.

Before allowing himself to relax, Torven pulled a bundle out of his pack. He snapped one of the thick, black sticks and a flame erupted from the center. He set it down and arranged the other heat sticks around it, watching them alight as they touched the burning flame. The fire would burn for hours, without tending. It would keep them warm and deter creatures from their shelter.

He took a quick look around where he sat. No scat. It didn't mean there were no creatures in the cave, but at least, nothing had come to this entrance in a while.

Too exhausted to eat, Torven unfurled a blanket from one of the packs and covered Trista, then leaned back against the other pack. He crossed his legs and folded his arms, glancing down at the sleeping woman.

He brushed a strand of her hair off her face. She looked peaceful, with her eyes closed, and none of the fear dancing behind her eyes. She hadn't seemed scared of him when he'd been carrying her, and he hoped that meant she'd forgiven him for kidnapping her. It could have been the thinner air making her forget to be angry with him, but at this point, he'd take it.

He stroked a finger down her cheek as he watched her sleep, his own eyes feeling heavy. The last thought he had as he drifted off to sleep was that they were safe. No one could hurt her or take her from him. For now.

CHAPTER
TWELVE

Trista rolled over, and her face touched something cold. She blinked and opened her eyes, discovering that her cheek was pressed against the ground. Although the hard rock wasn't covered with ice, it was frigid.

Where was she? A few feet away, a pile of black sticks burned low, and gave off a yellow glow of light and some blessed warmth. From the fire's dim illumination, she could see she was lying in a cave of some kind. She rubbed her head, trying to remember how she'd gotten there.

The last thing she could remember, she'd been running across icy terrain. The shuttle. She remembered the shuttle, and watching it sink beneath the surface of the ice. Her stomach tightened. That's right. They were stranded on the frozen planet. Their only way off was probably at the bottom of an icy lake, along with some seriously scary creatures.

She shuddered. She could go a lifetime without ever laying eyes on that freaky albino monster again. That is, if she had a lifetime. She couldn't imagine surviving for long in a place with no vegetation, and no animals that didn't want to devour them. At least,

Torven had seriously wounded that mutant alligator and kept it from taking a bite out of her.

Torven. Her pulse fluttered. Where was Torven? He'd been running beside her. Hadn't he carried her at some point?

She sat up and peered through the dim lighting, but didn't see him. She heard a noise behind her and spun. He was slumped against a wall of the cave, his arms crossed and his head lolled to one side. For a moment, she worried that he wasn't breathing until she quieted her own breath and heard his slow, soft exhalations.

Even though he reminded her of a sleeping giant, his presence comforted her. Since he was asleep, she could really look at him without feeling like she was ogling him. And this time she didn't have to feel guilty for gaping at him like she did after she shot him.

Like every Drexian warrior she'd seen, he was big. But not just bulky, like some of the men she'd known back home who'd let muscle go to fat. Every inch of him was hard muscle. She could see that even through the form-fitting environmental suit, and she'd felt it when he'd pinned her down.

She realized that he was actually quite handsome, when his eyebrows weren't furrowed with worry and his eyes weren't burning with anger. She liked the dark scruff on his face and the black lining his eyes, although the plunge in the lake appeared to have worn off most of the pigment.

She shivered as a blast of cold air blew into the cave and seemed to go right through her suit. Looking down, Trista noticed a tear in the fabric near her stomach.

It must have gotten ripped when I fell into the ice, she thought. Since she'd been sleeping with her back to the entrance, she hadn't felt the cold, but now the air chilled her skin.

Trista turned fully toward Torven, sidling as close as she could to share his body heat. He jerked as he woke, fumbling for his blaster until he saw it was just her sitting next to him.

His eyes swept the cave. "Are you okay?" He tilted his head at her. "You weren't planning on shooting me in my sleep, were you?"

She tried to give him an outraged look, but it ended up a half-smile. "I told you I was sorry about that, and I promised never to do it again. Anyway, it would be pretty shitty to shoot the guy who saved my life."

"I am also the guy who kidnapped you," he said, his forehead creasing.

"I've decided to let that slide. I've also decided to believe that you're innocent."

His expression grew serious. "Thank you."

She shrugged. "You believed in me when I told you I could fix the ship. I figure I can return the favor and believe in you."

"The ship." He groaned like he'd just remembered everything that had happened.

"Yeah. So much for getting out of here." She rubbed her arms. "I did mention that I hate winter, right?"

"I promise this is not how our story ends," Torven said. "We will get out of here."

"I hate to be the one to remind you, but we're on a giant ball of ice with no ship. We were flying stealth when we crashed, and no one knows where we were heading."

"That is all true, but I sent a communication before we jumped off the ship."

"You did? Like an SOS?" Her voice dropped. "Doesn't that mean the Drexians will be able to find you and arrest you?"

"I sent it coded over a special channel only used by Inferno Force," Torven said. "There are few people who can intercept it, and even fewer who can decipher it."

Her shoulders slumped. "So, you're saying I shouldn't hold my breath for the rescue party?"

"I'm saying the rescue party will hopefully not be an arresting party."

"Let's hope Dorn can prove that you didn't do it. I'd kind of like to go home."

"Home to Iowa?" Torven asked, knowing that tribute brides

could not return to Earth.

She scrunched her mouth to one side. "That's funny. I was actually thinking about the station as home. I'm happy to never see Iowa again."

"No? It is not a pleasing place?"

She shrugged. "I'm sure it is for some. There's lots of nice farmland, some decent cities, and tons of free parking. I was just ready to get out."

"And now the Boat feels like home?"

She thought for a moment. "The crazy thing is, it does. I've been so focused on feeling like I didn't fit in there, but at this point there's no place I'd rather be. No offense to this place."

Torven managed a small grin. "I have been to many planets, and I would not count this among my favorites, although I would rather be here with you than anywhere else."

Trista's pulse tripped. "Yeah, whatever."

"You do not believe me?" Torven's expression was serious. "I would never lie to you. That would be dishonorable."

She met his eyes and the intensity of his gaze made her catch her breath. "Okay, I believe you. I'd still rather be back on the Boat." She dropped her eyes. "I thought by this point we'd both be there."

He pulled one of her hands into his. "Tell me more about the Boat."

"I know I've only been there for a few weeks, but my suite—our suite, I guess—is a holographic recreation of a Greek island, and it's pretty nice. It has a great view. I never would have been able to visit someplace as amazing as that if I'd stayed on Earth. And I really like the other tribute brides. At first, they intimidated me, but they've all been so nice to me. And I've even warmed up to the nutty aliens in charge of planning the weddings."

His eyes held hers. "Had you started planning our wedding?"

Trista swallowed hard, trying to quell the butterflies in her stomach. "I kept putting it off by saying I wanted to wait and see what you liked."

"But that wasn't the real reason?" he asked.

She dropped her gaze and let out a breath. "I didn't want to start planning, because I didn't want to get my hopes up. I haven't had the greatest track record with guys, and I wasn't sure you'd even want me once you met me."

Torven lifted her chin with one finger. "Why would you think I would not want you?"

His piercing stare made her cheeks burn. She bit the corner of her bottom lip. "I might not be what you expected. I know I'm not hot, and all you Drexians have these amazing, hard bodies and I... Well, I don't."

"I do not want you to look like my Drexian brothers." He traced his thumb along her jawline. "I like you soft."

Her skin buzzed where he touched her. "Oh."

"But you were right about one thing," he said. "You are not what I expected. I never imagined that you would be courageous enough to shoot me or that you would be a...What did you call it? A grease monkey?"

She couldn't help grinning. "I don't think whoever picked me out on Earth imagined that, either."

"You have been a very good surprise." He ran his finger down her throat and paused. "You are shivering. Are you cold?"

She motioned to the rip in her suit. "I must have torn it earlier."

Torven began unzipping his suit. "You will wear mine."

She waved him off. "No way. I don't want you to freeze to death." She hesitated for a moment then crawled into his lap. "This will be better."

His entire body went rigid as she straddled him, pressing her chest flush with his and wrapping her legs around his waist. She didn't know if it was the fact that she knew they'd probably die stranded on the planet, or if it was the fact that he'd risked his life for her more than once, but Trista felt safer the closer she was to him. Not only that, she wanted him. Bad. She'd heard the other tribute brides talk about their hot and horny guys. Now she had one right next to her—and one who desired her—and she wasn't going to let fear or her stupid past ruin it for her.

She'd never been the aggressive one when it came to relationships, seeming to trip and fall into bad guys who liked to take control. She liked the idea of calling the shots for once, even if her entire body shook at the thought of seducing Torven.

"Body heat," she said as she leaned her face against his chest and heard his rapid heartbeat. "It will keep us warm while we sleep."

He didn't say anything in response, and Trista hoped she hadn't read him wrong and made a huge mistake.

CHAPTER THIRTEEN

Torven closed his eyes and blew out a breath. How was he supposed to sleep like this? Her body was pressed against him, and he could feel the soft swell of her breasts and the curve of her ass.

It was warmer, he'd give her that, although he couldn't say if it was shared body heat, or the fact that her touch sent fire rocketing through him. She shifted, and he swallowed a groan.

No matter how slowly he breathed in and out, his cock pulsed between his legs. It didn't help that she was straddling him, the only thing between them a few layers of fabric. Her full breasts pressed up against his chest, making him bite his lip to keep from sliding his hands up her body. He swallowed the sharp tang of blood.

"It would work better if you wrapped your arms around me," Trista said.

Was this still about body heat? He couldn't see her face, so he couldn't tell if she was deliberately arousing him. It didn't matter. He had no right to claim her. Not yet. Not until he was free.

"Torven?" she said, her tone insistent. "Arms."

He circled his arms around her, leaning his head back against the rock of the cave wall. It's just for warmth, he told himself. *We need to stay warm.*

Torven tried to ignore her when she raised her head and nuzzled his neck. It was clear she was exhausted, and suffering the effects of the thinner atmosphere. He steeled himself and thought back to particularly gruesome battles he'd fought in. If he kept his eyes closed and ignored the flowery scent of her hair, he could almost imagine himself on his Inferno Force battleship, the air filled with the sound of explosions and the smell of burning fuel.

His mind wandered from his memories to the feel of the soft female wiggling in his lap. Gods, this was harder than he'd thought.

No matter how desperately he wanted to flip her onto her back, rip off her suit, and claim her lush body, he knew he could not. Not until he was proven innocent. He may be a disgraced Drexian warrior, but he still had his honor, and he would not take what wasn't his to take.

Torven comforted himself with the thought that his friends would be working to prove that he was not a traitor. Soon, he would be vindicated and the pretty human would be his. Until then, he would have to grit his teeth and fight his urges.

"If we ever get off this barren planet."

"What?" her question made his eyes open.

Had he said that out loud? "Nothing. Just hoping my transmission got out before the ship went under."

Trista traced a finger over the flat, ebony tooth that hung from the leather string around his neck and rested in the hollow of his throat. "I'm assuming this isn't a shark's tooth, since I'm guessing there aren't necessarily sharks on other planets."

He answered without looking down. "It is a craktow tooth. From the planet Grandor."

"What does a craktow look like?"

This was good. Thinking about alien beasts took his mind off his aching cock. "Its skin is as black as its tooth, and it swims under the water. It is the size of at least three Drexians and has serrated fins."

Trista shuddered. “So, like a shark on steroids.”

He did not know what that meant, so he grunted in reply.

“Did you kill it to get the tooth?” she asked.

He nodded, touching the tooth absently. “I was not alone. It took many of us to bring it down, and we almost drowned.”

She put her hand over his as he fingered the tooth, then she lowered her hand to rub it across the muscles of his chest. “Torven?”

“Yes?” He heard the huskiness in his voice.

“What if we don’t get off this planet?” she asked. “What if we’re stuck here?”

He flinched as she put words to his fear. “Someone will find us. My people will not give up looking for you, if nothing else.”

“But without any sort of black box or beacon, what are the chances they’ll come looking on this popsicle of a planet?”

He wasn’t sure what she meant by ‘black box’ or ‘popsicle.’ “My brothers from Inferno Force will hear my transmission,” he said with more confidence than he felt. “They will find us.”

Her breath was warm against his neck, and his cock twitched. She was not making this easy.

She nipped at his neck. “You sure?”

“Trista.” He dropped his hands to her hips as she arched them forward, rocking against his hard cock. Blood pounded in his ears as he fought his desire.

“Yes, Torven?” She looked up at him, her eyes wide.

He loved hearing her say his name. He wanted to hear her screaming it as he made her come.

“Not like this,” he said, forcing the words out of his mouth.

“No?” Her tone was teasing as she dragged her tongue down his neck and then tugged on the craktow tooth with her teeth. She leaned back, running a hand down his chest and he caught it before she reached his cock.

“What’s wrong?” She pulled back. “I thought you wanted me.”

“I can’t,” he said.

Her cheeks became splotched with color. "Can't? Or don't want to?"

"You don't understand," he said, releasing his grip on her hand.

She scrambled off him. "Oh, I think I understand being lied to pretty well."

He stared at her as she scooted away from him and pulled her knees up to her chest. "Lied to?"

Her breath was ragged. "I'm sure it's easier to keep me subdued if you tricked me into thinking you're into me, right? Make the stupid human fall for you, and then she won't try to run off, is that it?"

Torven watched as she shrank into herself, her shoulders slumping forward and her eyes swimming with tears. He shook his head. "That's not what I was..."

She held out a hand, her palm toward him. "Save me the explanations. I've heard them all. It all boils down to me being an idiot again." Her voice became a whisper. "I don't know why I ever believed someone like you would be into me anyway."

Torven felt a flash of anger at the human men who'd made his mate feel this way about herself, and at himself for managing to hurt her when all he wanted to do was keep her safe. Before she could stop him, he'd pulled her back to him.

She squealed in surprise as Torven flipped her underneath him, his lower body pinning her to the floor and his cock hard and pressed between her legs.

"Does this feel like I do not want you?"

Trista blinked a few times. "Torven."

"Yes, mate." He ground himself into her. "I want to hear you say my name just like that when my cock is buried deep inside you. Actually, I want to ride you so hard you scream my name over and over."

He saw the confusion in her eyes replaced by a flicker of heat as she arched into him.

Desire arrowed through him as his restraint crumbled. He put one hand under her round ass and jerked her closer as she lifted a leg and hooked it around his waist. He lowered his mouth to hers, savoring the taste of her as his tongue parted her lips.

She sighed as she sank into the kiss, yielding to him and caressing his tongue with hers. Torven moaned at the touch and ground his cock into her. Desire roared through him, making his head swim as she writhed underneath him. He knew he should stop, but everything about her felt right. His need to claim her drowned out every reasonable thought he'd ever had about honor.

Through the rushing of blood in his head, he heard something that made him stop. Reluctantly, he pulled away and put a finger to her lips. Her heavy breathing filled his ears, but he listened for the sound again.

Footsteps. Coming closer.

His gut clenched. It was too soon for Inferno Force to have reached them.

The heavy, crunching steps echoing through the rocks indicated more than one person. A search party. But not a rescue party. If Torven's instincts were right, they were not Drexian.

CHAPTER FOURTEEN

Trista stifled a yelp of surprise as Torven yanked her up and jerked his head toward the spokes of the cave that extended deeper into the mountain. Even though he had to bend when he stood, her head only grazed the ceiling, although she wasn't sure how roomy the tunnels would be. She eyed their darkness with suspicion.

"We must run," he whispered

For a moment, she was annoyed. Her body buzzed with arousal, the heat from his touch lingering. Before she could ask him what he was talking about and why he'd stopped, she heard the rhythmic thudding on the ground. She felt a surge of confusion and then relief as she registered the noises. Footsteps. Someone had found them. They were saved. Then she saw Torven's face, and her gut clenched. "Those aren't your friends, are they?"

He shook his head, his mouth set in a thin line. He moved deeper into the cave, pulling her with him.

"What about our things?" Trista asked, resisting being dragged away even as the footfall grew louder. "If they see them, it will confirm we're here."

Torven scooped up the black heat rods, twisting them to douse them, and dropping them into his open pack while Trista grabbed the blanket and jammed it into her pack, hooking the bag over one shoulder.

She hesitated as she glanced at the tunnels extending out from the cave. "Which one?"

Torven didn't hesitate before picking the one to the far left and taking off at a bent-over jog with one of her hands in his and his other hand on the wall for guidance. Trista's heart raced as they went farther into the dark tunnel, and she stayed as close to Torven as she could without tripping him.

No light extended into the tunnel. They were too deep into the rocks, and too far away from the mouth of the cave. It was so dark, she couldn't see Torven, even though he was inches from her.

"Don't we have a headlamp or something?" she whispered as she stumbled over a bit of uneven rock.

"We do not, but they would see it, anyway," he replied.

It's fine, she told herself as she tried to keep her instinctive fear of the dark at bay. This is better than being caught by whoever came for us. At least she hoped it was. She was trusting Torven on that one.

She couldn't hear the footsteps anymore, which she hoped meant the search party wasn't in pursuit. They'd have no way of knowing which of the several tunnels she and Torven had taken, even if they did determine they'd been in the cave, which she doubted they would.

The only noise came from their light footfall and their breath. After a few minutes, Torven stopped and pulled her close and held one hand over her mouth. She knew he was listening, so she held her breath.

Rough, guttural sounds were a distant echo. They'd found the cave, and it sounded like the creatures were arguing. Torven stiffened as he listened.

"Kronock," he said in her ear, his voice barely audible as he dropped his hand from her mouth.

"You mean the aliens who are trying to invade Earth?" she whispered back.

"Yes." He did not sound happy.

Trista could feel his body rigid beside her. She guessed she couldn't blame him. What was the sworn enemy of the Drexians doing here, and how had they found them faster than anyone else?

Torven gave her arm a quick tug and they started moving again, this time walking. She was amazed by how softly he could tread considering how huge he was. Trista followed him on her toes.

The tunnel sloped down, and the air became colder and staler. She shivered and hoped they were moving toward an exit, although she suspected they were simply going deeper and deeper into the ground. Trista tried not to think about the tons of rock overhead, or the possibility of being trapped under it. She'd never been claustrophobic, but she'd also never been inside a rock tunnel under a mountain in the pitch dark.

She didn't know how long they'd been walking, when the tunnel began to angle up again. Despite her heavy pack and burning legs, she picked up the pace and squeezed Torven's hand. Going up had to be a good thing, right?

Trista's toe caught on a ridge in the floor and she pitched forward, giving a small yelp before Torven caught her.

His entire body went rigid as he held her and they both listened. The pounding of feet followed yells farther back down the tunnel.

Shit. They'd heard. Torven yanked her up and they both started running. Trista wanted to kick herself. She knew it had been instinct that had made her cry out, but now they were going to be blown away, all because she couldn't stay quiet.

You're so stupid, Trista. The words filled her head before she could stop them. How many times had she heard that? She shook her head as they ran, feeling tears prick the backs of her eyes, and she attempted to ignore the voice in her head. She hated that she could still hear the echoes of her ex-boyfriend, as if he stood next to her. Every time she felt bad about herself, she could count on Rick to show up. Not that she could count on any of her exes when they'd been together.

Her lungs burned as the tunnel became steeper. It felt like Torven was dragging her up the incline, as the sounds behind them became louder. The enemy was gaining on them, and she knew it was because she was too slow.

"You should leave me behind," she said, her words short bursts between breaths.

"No."

"Torven," she said, hearing the desperation in her own voice, "I'm slowing you down. Without me, you can escape."

A grunt was his only reply.

Trista almost wept. She was going to get them both captured, and he was too stubborn to admit it.

She looked up to plead with him some more to leave her, and she realized she could see the outline of his hair. A tiny bit of light trickled into the tunnel from up ahead. They were almost to the end. There was an end. She sucked in her breath and powered forward.

Torven glanced down at her, and she could make out a faint smile. The smile vanished a moment later as blaster fire hit the wall next to them.

Trista ducked but didn't slow her pace. They had to get out. She refused to die in a tunnel.

Torven pushed her in front of him and pulled his blaster from his waist, firing back over his shoulder.

She couldn't tell how far the Kronock were from them, since the tunnel was a cacophony of voices and blaster shots echoing back on each other. The opening of the cavern was within sight now. Trista dashed for it, desperate to be outside in the freezing cold surrounded by ice again. She didn't know how much better things would be for them once they were out in the open, but it had to be better than a narrow tunnel filled with blaster fire.

She burst out of the mountain and found herself staring at a vast stretch of ice and snow, with nowhere to hide. So much for things being better once they got out. She spun around to ask Torven where they should go, but he was standing outside the mouth of the tunnel, blasting at the rock face above it.

Trista staggered back as slabs of granite broke off above the opening, and crashed down in front of it. The voices inside grew louder, as Torven continued to fire. More rock sheared off, and the pile at the tunnel's opening grew.

Blaster fire emerged from the top of the rock pile, and Trista ducked out of the way. The Kronock were firing from inside, but Torven's landslide of boulders kept falling. When there was only a sliver of space at the top, he stopped shooting and bent over, putting his hands on his knees.

"You will answer for this, Drexian," a Kronock voice screamed from behind the rocks.

"You're really racking up the enemies," she said.

Torven chuckled, then winced as he stood. Since they were outside and surrounded by ice and snow, their environmental suits were now white. Which meant the red splotch on his side was bright against the starkness.

She rushed to him. "You're hurt."

He touched a hand to the wound, and it came away covered with sticky blood. "I will be fine. We need to put some distance between us and the Kronock."

"There's no point in escaping them if you drop dead in the process," she said.

Torven frowned. "I will not drop dead."

"Pigheaded," Trista said, shaking her head.

"Pig? What is pig?"

She rolled her eyes. "It means you're stubborn."

Torven took a step and cringed, clearly in pain. "Should I remind you that you also shot me?" He held up two fingers. "Twice."

She let out a breath. She was never going to live that down. "I may have changed my mind about you. It's a woman's prerogative. And now it's my prerogative to make sure you don't die on me." She pressed a hand to his wound.

Torven grimaced from the pressure. "I think I preferred it when you were attempting to kill me."

CHAPTER FIFTEEN

Torven leaned against the frigid boulder, breathing in the icy air and holding his hand over his wound as Trista had instructed him. The warmth of his blood was a sharp contrast to the cold, and he tried to ignore the metallic scent of it as it trickled between his fingers.

They had decided to wind back into the mountains and search for another cave where they could hide from the Kronock. But not before Trista had insisted on running out onto the icy tundra and leaving a trail to throw off their pursuers.

Torven scanned the white landscape, his stomach tight with worry. He'd argued against her leaving him, but of course, she hadn't listened. She seemed to have doubled her confidence since he'd met her, going from terrified to headstrong. If this was his doing, he would need to rethink things. Her newfound courage made him uneasy. It was one thing for him to risk his life, but he did not want his mate to be in danger. Even if it meant saving his life.

As she appeared from around the curve in the rocks, he released his breath, but did not stop scowling. "You were gone too long. You said it would only take a few minutes."

"Sorry," she said. "I wanted to leave a convincing trail."

He glanced at the blanket she held, and the one blood-soaked corner. "And my blood?"

"It should lead them far away from us." Trista wrapped the blanket into a ball and jammed it back in one of the packs. She hiked the pack on her back and slipped an arm around Torven's waist. "Let's see if we can find another decent cave."

They made their way up into the mountains, careful to go in the direction away from where they'd left the Kronock barricaded in the tunnel. Torven tried not to lean on Trista, but his side ached where he'd been shot, and he knew he was losing blood with each step.

After he stumbled for the third time, Trista stopped. "That's it. Enough with the tough-guy act. We need to take care of your wound."

He shook his head. "Not until we find shelter."

Trista slipped out from under his arm, crossed her own arms, and tapped one toe on the ground. "Good luck walking without me."

He held her gaze and then let out an exasperated sigh. "Fine, but let's be quick." He leaned against the rock face and dropped his backpack. "The med kit should be in here."

Trista took the bag from him and began pawing through it. "So, what are the chances that the sworn enemy of your people just happened to turn up here?"

Torven closed his eyes as his head swam. "Low. They aren't here by accident."

Trista pulled out the med kit and popped it open. She squatted on the ground to examine the contents. "You think they followed us here?"

"I cannot say for certain, but I can think of no other reason for them to be on this planet."

"Oh, I don't know," Trista said. "The scenery is quite nice. I'm thinking about building a summer home here."

He opened his eyes and saw her smirking up at him. "One of your jokes?"

She nodded, straightening up. "I take it you've never seen *The Princess Bride*?"

"Is this a royal person on your planet?"

She laughed. "No, it's a...Never mind. It doesn't matter. You don't think they just happened to see us heading for the planet and followed us?"

He grunted as she approached him with a medical scanner and a few shiny packets he recognized as disinfectant. "We were using stealth technology. The fact that the Kronock are here tells me that the real traitor is still feeding them information. That's the only way they could know I escaped the station. The Drexian traitor told them, and they managed to track us, or intercept my transmission."

"Why do you think they're trying to kill you?" Trista asked. "Wasn't framing you bad enough?"

"They probably thought I would have been tried and convicted by now." Torven's mind whirled. "The longer I survive, the more of a chance that their entire plan is exposed."

Her mouth fell open. "So, they *have* to get rid of you?"

He gave a single nod. "I think so. Which is why we must hide."

Trista seemed to snap out of her shock. "Right. As soon as I stop your bleeding. We don't want to leave an actual trail for the Kronock to follow, and right now you're bleeding like a stuck pig."

"Again with the pig," Torven said. "Are these pigs very important on your world?"

"They are if you like bacon." Trista grinned, clearly amused by her own comment. "Now take off your suit."

He gingerly unzipped the top and shrugged one shoulder out, flinching as he tried the other side.

"Let me help." Trista put down the medical scanner and gently tugged at the remaining arm of the suit, her fingers brushing his skin.

He stopped moving and watched her pull his environmental suit down until it hung around his waist. He knew she was doing it to help treat his injury, but the sight of her small hands peeling clothes away from his body made his chest thrum. Even the barest brush of her knuckles against his exposed flesh caused his heart to beat faster.

She lifted his shirt and bent over to get a better look at the blaster wound in his side. Torven followed her gaze. Blood had dried around the blast mark, but fresh blood continued to trickle from the opening.

"I need to clean it first." She tore open one of the disinfectant packets and rubbed the clear solution over her hands first. Then she squeezed the rest into one palm and applied her hand to his side.

Torven jerked from the cold solution and from the initial sting as it sanitized his skin.

She looked up at him, her brows pressed together. "You okay?"

He nodded without speaking. Warriors should not acknowledge pain or weakness, but he felt the burn all the way to his toes. He slid an arm around her waist and pulled her flush against him. She didn't move her hand from his wound, but feeling her warmth made him breathe easier. He bent down so her head tucked in under his chin.

She relaxed into him for a second. "Um, Torven? I kind of need to stitch you up." She tilted her head to peer up at him. "You aren't stalling, are you?"

He shook his head. He wasn't a fan of medical treatments, preferring to grit his way through injury, but he'd never admit that to her. "You do not like me holding you?"

"I do, but I also want to get you fixed up." She cocked an eyebrow at him. "I'd hate for you to be too weak to walk or to..."

She let her words trail off, and heat coursed through his body as he understood her meaning. He didn't think it would be possible for him to be too weak for that, but he didn't want to find out. He straightened up. "I'm ready."

Trista removed her hand from his side and examined the scanner. "So, if I'm right, this should seal you up."

Torven put a hand on her wrist. "Do you know how to use this?"

Her eyes darted to the small metal device. "I think so. Once Mandy showed me how to, when she gave me a tour of the medical bay back on the station."

"Once?"

Trista cocked an eyebrow at him. "Yes, once. Would you prefer we wait for a fully-trained doctor to fix you up?"

Torven knew he could not wait. He already felt weak from all the blood he'd lost. He lowered his hand and gave her a half grin. "You are sure this is not another attempt to kill me?"

"Was that a joke, Torven?" She smiled. "I told you I've abandoned my plans to knock you off. You're growing on me."

Warmth bloomed in his chest that had nothing to do with the burning sensation in his side.

"Besides, I kind of need you to survive this place," she added, aiming the scanner at him and pressing a button.

He twitched as a green beam shot from the end and started to seal his torn flesh. It didn't hurt, but it sent a warm tingle through his body.

"Hold still," Trista said, her eyes focused intently on his side. "Almost done."

Watching his own skin knitting together was an odd thing to observe. He looked away, until he heard the device click off.

Trista beamed at him and waved a hand at his newly healed side. "As good as new."

Torven touched a finger to the pink patch on his flesh. It was still tender, but there was no scar.

"Drexian technology really is impressive." Trista flipped the scanner around in her palm. "I wish there were devices like this to fix cars."

Torven shrugged his suit back up over his shoulders. "You are a curious female."

"I'm okay with that." Trista's mouth curved up as she returned the scanner and used packets to the med kit, and hiked the pack up onto her back. "We need to get you someplace where you can rest."

"I am fine." He picked up his own pack as he pulled himself up to his full height, and black spots danced in front of his eyes. He swayed on the spot, throwing his arms out as he staggered to one side.

"Torven!" Her voice cut through the roaring in his ears. "You're too close to the edge."

He tried to stop himself, but the world was a swirl of white as he fell, his arms catching nothing but empty air.

CHAPTER SIXTEEN

Trista dove for Torven as he listed to one side near the edge of the path. No way was she losing him after working so hard to keep him alive, and no way was he leaving her alone on a frozen planet.

His arms windmilled as he realized he was falling, and Trista clutched one of his hands in an attempt to stop his momentum. He clasped her hand and his weight yanked them both off the ledge.

Shit. Air rushed by her as they plummeted down. She was too startled to scream, even as panic clawed at her throat. She couldn't believe that after everything she'd survived, this was how she was going out. She tightened her grip on Torven's hand, and closed her eyes.

The impact was softer than she'd expected, with clouds of snow flying into the air around them as they landed. Torven took the fall on his back, and she bounced on top of him, the only pain coming when her head knocked against his.

She lay still for a moment, savoring the fact that she wasn't dead. She ran a hand over her upper body. It didn't feel like anything was broken, either.

"Torven?" she whispered as she pushed herself off his chest. "Are you okay?"

He groaned. "You pushed me off the mountain."

"Pushed you?" She slapped his chest. "I was trying to save you, you big—" She stopped when she noticed the grin playing around the corners of his mouth. She slapped him again, this time harder. "I *should* push you off the mountain."

He opened one eye and peeked at her. "How many times have you tried to kill me now?"

"Not enough," she said, but couldn't help laughing.

"If we ever get off this planet, remind me not to arm you."

Trista sat up completely and glanced around. She was so relieved they weren't dead, she couldn't even be upset that they'd fallen so far that they'd lost all their progress into the mountain range. The pile of soft snow they'd landed in was at the base of the craggy rock face.

She sighed. It would take hours to retrace their steps, even if Torven was strong enough to walk that far. She'd led the Kronock away from them, but that only gave them a head start. It wouldn't take long for the enemy to discover the trail was false and circle back around.

"We still need to find someplace to hide," she said.

Torven pushed himself up onto his elbows. "We're almost back to where we started."

Trista heard the weariness in his voice. No way could he hack another hike up the mountain. She wasn't sure if she could, either. The adrenaline was wearing off, and a chill passed through her body.

"I have an idea," she said, standing up and brushing the powdery snow off her suit. She tugged Torven up with her. "We go back to the tunnel. The Kronock will never think we're there, because they chased us out. I'm guessing they've blasted their way out by now, so we can circle back and hide inside."

Torven's forehead creased into a mass of wrinkles as he seemed to consider her idea. "It's an interesting strategy."

Trista didn't say aloud what she was thinking. It was risky, but it was their only decent option considering Torven's state, and the position of the tiny sun in the sky. Soon it would be dark again, and she did not want to be stuck outside when the temperature dropped even farther.

Torven took the lead, holding his blaster in front and moving slowly, as they navigated the short distance back to the tunnel. They didn't encounter anyone, or hear the sounds of a hunting party. Maybe her distraction had worked, and the enemy was wandering out in the snow searching for them.

They approached the entrance to the tunnel with trepidation, but it appeared to be deserted. The stones he'd caused to fall over the entrance were blasted away, as they'd suspected. He stepped over the rubble to reach the dark hole.

"Ready?" he asked, peering into the blackness and looking back at her.

Trista hadn't gone to church since she was a girl, but she said a silent prayer that no Kronock were waiting for them inside. "Let's do it."

As they shuffled hand in hand along the narrow passageway, Trista thought it was steeper than she remembered. They were walking down a lot, which meant that they would have been walking up coming from the opposite direction. Had they really walked up for so long before? Since they had been pursued earlier, Trista guessed the stress must have muddled the details. Her ears popped, and she gave her head a shake.

Instead of becoming cooler as they descended, Trista could swear it was warmer. And humid. She took a deep breath. Yep, the air smelled damp, if that was possible. She took another breath, picking up a hint of rotten eggs.

"Torven," she whispered. "Do you smell that?"

"This is not the same tunnel," he said, putting voice to her suspicion. "There must have been a fork in it we weren't aware of."

It was still too dark to see anything, but Trista squeezed Torven's hand. "How far are we going to go? It may not come out on the other side."

"Up ahead."

Trista squinted through the dark. He was right. There was a faint, blue glow in the distance. As they drew nearer, the blue light grew brighter until they came out of the tunnel into a subterranean cavern. Tiny flecks of blue glowed in the walls, and stalactites extended from the high ceiling with matching stalagmites reaching up from the floor.

From the faint light emitted from the walls, Trista could see that the cave was large, with columns throughout that appeared to have been formed from dripping minerals. It looked like rock had been poured down in globs, or cobbled together out of icicles. In the center of the cavern was a pool of water, with steam rising from its surface.

"I must be hallucinating," Trista said. "Either that, or we actually died, and this is heaven."

Torven lowered his blaster as he walked forward and touched one of the hanging needles of damp rock. "It feels real."

Trista walked to the edge of the pool and leaned over, dipping her hand into the water. "It's warm." She pulled it out and sniffed her fingers. "This must be a natural spring deep within the planet. The water smells like sulfur."

Torven wrinkled his nose. "It is healthy to breathe?"

"It's fine, I think," Trista said. "If it's anything like on Earth, it's actually good for your skin. I had a cousin who went to Hot Springs, Arkansas, for her honeymoon, that's why I know. She couldn't stop talking about soaking in the natural springs."

Torven shrugged himself out of the environmental suit, lowered himself to the rock floor, and leaned his back against one of the lumpy formations. He blew out a steady breath, and flinched as he held a hand to his side.

Trista studied him. He must be in pain. She knew what she'd done to patch him up wasn't a permanent fix, and she didn't know if he had internal injuries. Her heart squeezed when she thought about something happening to him, but she gave herself a mental shake. First of all, why was she so worried about someone she barely knew? Aside from the fact that she always fell for the wrong type of guy, of course.

She watched him with his eyes closed and his head resting against the craggy rock. He wasn't so intimidating when he looked like he was sleeping. Sure, he still had a face full of dark scruff, and thick tattoos ringing his biceps, but his square jaw and full lips softened his look. It didn't hurt that he'd risked his own life to save hers.

Maybe he was just doing a really good job of convincing her, but her gut told her he'd never intentionally put her at risk. She knew she should still be upset that he took her from the station and landed her on a frozen planet with nothing but terrifying monsters trying to kill them and Kronock chasing after them, but it was hard to stay angry at someone when they kept saving your life and you were fighting off the urge to jump their bones.

No one back home would have been surprised by this, she reminded herself as a rush of shame flooded her cheeks. It had become a given that if there was a bad boy within fifty feet, Trista would be drawn to him like a moth to a flame. Of course, none of the bad boys she'd liked had ever turned out to be nice guys underneath. They'd all been jerks who'd made her feel like crap, which was why she'd vowed never to so much as look at one again. Being taken to outer space had helped, and then she'd seen Torven, and all of her good intentions had gone out the window.

Of all the Drexian warriors available, how was it she got stuck with the bad-boy outcast? She knew they'd been matched, but she could reject the match, especially since Torven might end up a convicted traitor. All she had to do was resist him until they were rescued, go back to the station, and ask for a clean-cut soldier with no tattoos. Her eyes fell to his broad chest, the black shirt pulled tight over his sculpted muscles, and a throbbing heat pulsed between her legs. Easier said than done.

She shifted as the uncomfortable warmth became a tingle. Had she really learned nothing from her past? As much as she tried to fight it, she knew she was falling for the rough-around-the-edges warrior.

"Typical," she muttered under her breath.

He looked up as her soft word echoed through the cavern. "What?"

"Nothing," she stammered. "Maybe we should get you in the water. It might help your wounds."

Torven raised a suspicious eyebrow and eyed the steaming pool. "Are you sure this is not another of your ploys to do away with me?"

"By making you soak in a natural hot tub?" She laughed. "If so, there are worse ways to go."

The corner of Torven's mouth quirked up. "Maybe you are running out of other ways."

She shrugged. "Don't tell me you're scared of a woman?"

He seemed to take this as a challenge, standing and pulling his shirt over his head in one fluid movement. He smiled at her. "I am not scared of you, *cinnara*."

"Cinnara?"

"It means 'my sweet one.' I could also call you the other name. What was it? Grease monkey?"

Trista didn't know how to respond. She'd never had a cute nickname, unless you considered being called 'woman' endearing, which she didn't.

Torven didn't wait for her answer as he stepped out of his pants, leaving them in a pile on the ground. She knew this was the point where she should look away, but she couldn't tear her eyes from him. There were those nodes again, she thought, as she got a quick glimpse of the row of bumps along his spine. She'd seen him in just his boxer briefs before, but her breath hitched in her throat as he also pulled those off and tossed them aside.

The other tribute brides on the station had told her that Drexians weren't as modest as humans, and they didn't have any problem stripping in front of virtual strangers. Now she knew why. If human men looked like Torven, she was sure they'd be parading naked in front of as many people as they could. Hell, they'd probably take out full-page ads. They'd need a full page to do it justice.

She knew she shouldn't stare, but she'd never seen such a huge cock in her life. Not that it came as a surprise. Everything about Torven was massive, and she'd felt his girth pressing against her leg earlier and suspected as much. Still, seeing it was different than imagining it. Thick and long, it was as bronze as his skin with the crown only a shade darker.

Trista watched as he poked one toe in the water then lowered himself completely. He submerged himself under the surface before rising up from the water and sweeping water off his face and dragging his hands through his hair. Water beaded off his chest and streamed down his tattooed arms.

She felt a spasm between her legs. Holy shit. Was this guy for real? It was like living a perfume ad, with the sexy guy emerging from the water to tell you to buy a bottle of whatever he was selling.

He leveled his gaze at her. "Don't make me drag you in."

CHAPTER SEVENTEEN

Torven watched as Trista's cheeks flamed red, and he knew it wasn't just because of the heat. He'd heard that humans were more self-conscious about being naked than Drexians, but he thought after the moment they'd shared in the cave and the fact that she'd seen him almost naked before, she wouldn't be so modest.

It was true he hadn't seen her unclothed, but even the thought of seeing her naked curves made his cock twitch. He splashed some of the warm water up onto his bare chest and watched the last traces of blood dissolve. She'd been right about the water. It seemed to revive him, and his muscles relaxed from the heat.

Trista took off her boots and rolled up the legs of her environmental suit. "I'll just get my feet wet first."

Torven lowered himself into the steaming water again, and the knots in his shoulders unwound. The water may have smelled funny, but there was no doubt it was helping him recover.

Sitting on the edge of the pool, Trista dangled her legs into the water. She watched Torven, but he could tell she was doing her best to avoid looking beneath the water's surface.

Glowing blue flecks, like the ones in the rock walls, illuminated the pool from within. The water was so clear that even in the eerie blue light, it would've been hard not to notice Torven's huge erection. He tried to ignore it himself, as he ducked his head under the water and let the heat envelop him.

He knew he shouldn't be thinking about claiming her until he could prove his innocence. It had been a promise he'd made to himself, but one that was becoming harder and harder to keep. He hadn't anticipated how much he would want her, or how impossible it was to be near her without wanting to touch her.

At least she was making it easier for him, staying out of the water and keeping the oversized suit on. He focused on the floppy fabric bunched around her knees, and hoped that would make his cock stop throbbing.

"Screw this," Trista muttered under her breath. She stood and started to strip.

So much for getting rid of his arousal, Torven thought. He didn't know if it was more polite to avert his eyes, but he couldn't pull his gaze from her.

Wiggling her hips as she slipped the suit off and stepped out of it, Trista didn't glance at him as she shimmied out of the clothes beneath the suit. When she stood in nothing but small, black panties and a matching bra, she hesitated. "Turn around," she said.

He started to laugh, but saw she was serious. "You do not wish me to see you?"

"I know we're supposed to be matched and all, but I still just met you, and I'm not used to stripping for guys I barely know."

He wondered if this had to do with her ridiculous idea of not being attractive enough. She'd let it slip in the cave, but he'd hoped his enthusiasm over her small, soft body had convinced her that was not the case. Torven wanted to argue that he knew her, that he'd been thinking about nothing but her for weeks, that he could not imagine a more desirable female, but he did not. If his mate was shy, he would look away. He pivoted so he faced the other direction and after a few moments, he heard the splash as she entered the pool.

"Okay," she said. "You can turn around."

She'd removed her remaining clothes, and lowered herself nearly all the way in the water. Despite the damp heat, Torven's mouth went dry, as he saw the top of her round breasts bob in the water. She leaned back and dunked her hair into the water then sank down so that only her head was above the surface.

"Oh my God," she said. "This feels so good."

Torven was unable to speak. Knowing that her wet, naked body was within arm's reach had his heart racing and his cock rock hard.

She swam to the edge and hooked her elbows behind her so that only the tops of her breasts were out of the water, her pink nipples peeking out as the water ebbed and flowed. She stretched her feet out in front of her and kicked gently, dropping her head back and closing her eyes.

Torven knew the promises he made himself, but he also knew in his heart that this female was his. He'd known it from the moment he saw her image. He couldn't explain the connection he felt to her, especially before he'd even met her, but when he'd seen her on the station, his instincts had been confirmed. This light-haired female ignited something in him no one ever had, and after what they'd been through together, he was more certain than ever. It didn't matter what happened next. It didn't matter if he was convicted or found to be innocent. The only thing that mattered to him right now was being with her and claiming her as his.

He stood up in the water and it poured off his back. He took a step toward her, grabbing her feet and making her eyes fly open.

Trista's mouth gaped as she took him in. "What are you...?"

"You know what I am doing." He spread her legs and stepped forward putting his hands on her hips and tugging her away from the wall. She yelped as he slid his hands down to cup her ass and jerked her up into his arms.

She clutched his shoulders and wrapped her legs around his

waist, her expression going from startled to hesitant to aroused in the span of three heartbeats. He let his gaze drop to the glistening curves of her breasts, the pink nipples, hard and pressing into his chest and then to the soft swell of her belly, and the thin strip of wispy hair below. He groaned and crushed his mouth to hers, feeling the jolt as she kissed him back, hard.

She let out a sigh as his tongue entwined with hers, and tightened her grip on him with her legs. Her hands dropped from his shoulders and wrapped around his back, her fingers finding his nodes.

The touch of her fingertips against his swollen bumps made him bow his back, wanting to feel more. She stroked up and down his spine with both hands, and his body shuddered.

"Am I doing this right?" she asked, pulling away for a moment. "Does this feel good?"

"Everything you do to me feels good.

She began circling the two nodes in the middle of his back with her fingers, and his knees nearly buckled. He'd never been touched like this before. Not by someone who made his heart constrict.

He ran one hand through her wet hair and pulled her mouth back to his. He loved the taste of her and the feel of her and was almost lightheaded at the sensations. He used his hands on her ass to push her up and drop his head so that he could capture one wet nipple in his mouth. He swirled his tongue around the hot nub then sucked on it as Trista writhed beneath him. Turning his attention to the other nipple, he nipped and sucked until he heard her whimper.

"Torven," she said, her voice high and breathy.

Hearing her say his name made what was left of his control crumble. His fingers bit into her ass as he ground her against him. He released her nipple with a final tug.

"Am I doing this right?" Torven asked, his voice teasing.

She used one hand to lift his face to hers. "I want to feel you inside me."

Desire arrowed through him. He captured her mouth again,

tasting her sweetness as his tongue delved deep and his mind whirled. There was nothing he wanted more than to bury his cock inside her, but he knew there was no turning back once he did. It would be one more crime to add to his list—taking a tribute bride who was not his.

He pulled back and looked at her big, blue eyes half-lidded with wanting. It didn't matter. Nothing mattered now, except this moment here with her and making her his own.

CHAPTER
EIGHTEEN

Trista felt dizzy as she met Torven's gaze. His eyes blazed, as he searched her own.

He cupped her jaw in one large hand and dragged his thumb across her lower lip. "You are sure you want this?"

Need stormed through her, almost knocking the breath out of her. She'd spent so long being unsure about everything—herself, her decisions, her judgment—but for some reason, she was sure about this. She was sure about him.

Trista knew it didn't make sense. She'd only known Torven for a matter of days. She couldn't really say she knew him at all, yet it seemed like she'd known him forever. There was something about the way he looked at her and teased her and took her teasing that made her feel sure. Surer than she'd ever been before.

Maybe she was being an idiot, convincing herself that a bad guy was actually good, but she couldn't fight her feelings or her need. Her entire body screamed out for him. She didn't care anymore if he was a bad guy or not. He was her bad guy.

Torven tipped her head up to his. "I need you to tell me."

She looked from his gold eyes to his full lips wet from kissing her. "Tell you...?"

He bent so his mouth was next to her ear. "Tell me you want me to fuck you."

The air rushed out of her, and her legs went boneless. She managed to nod.

He pulled back with a low growl. "Say it for me, beautiful."

Heat shot through her as she whispered the words. "Fuck me, Torven. I need you to fuck me hard."

He plundered her mouth, wrapping his arms around her and pulling her closer. His tongue stroked hers, and Trista felt like she was on fire, the desire pounding through her body nearly primal.

She rocked her hips into him, opening her legs wider and rubbing her clit against his corded stomach muscles. His hard cock bumped up against the crease of her ass.

Torven slid the hand on her ass so that his thick finger teased her opening. She let out a hoarse cry and jerked her hips down, demanding more. "Give it to me."

"Here?" He slid the tip of his finger inside and stopped.

Even his finger stretched her, but she needed more. She dropped her head back as her body quivered. Lowering her hand under the water, she slid her own finger inside herself, beside his, and let out a breath. "Right there."

Torven's pupils widened. "Where else, mate? Show me."

Trista grasped his shoulder with one hand and leaned back, looking down as she dragged her finger out and found her clit. Torven watched as she began working it, and a guttural sound escaped from deep in his throat. He sank his finger all the way inside her.

She didn't stop circling her clit as he pumped his finger in and out, the heat from the water making the sensations even sharper. She liked watching both their hands on her body. Before, she'd preferred sex in the dark, but now she wanted to watch him take her. She glanced at Torven's face, his jaw tight and his neck muscles straining as he watched his finger stroke inside her while she played with herself.

Trista's muscles contracted, squeezing his finger. She tore her eyes away and reared back as the orgasm barreled through her. Crying out as she jerked against him, she held onto his slick shoulder to keep from falling.

"Torven," she panted. "That was..."

"Only the beginning," he said, walking through the water to the edge of the pool and setting her down. He hooked her legs over his shoulders and dragged a hand from her neck down to the narrow strip of light-brown hair between her legs.

Her legs shook as she lay back, too satisfied to feel exposed, even though lying back with her legs up in the air was not something she usually liked. She normally would have had one hand draped across her belly or have been trying to suck it in, but none of those things mattered to her now.

Torven bent down in the water and moved her so her knees were over his shoulders. Trista's stomach somersaulted. Was he going down on her?

"You don't have to," she said.

"Have to?" His brows knitted together as if he was confused. "I have been waiting to taste my mate and lick her sweet juices."

Trista's skin tingled where he touched her. "Oh. Then don't let me stop you." She screwed up her courage and let her legs fall open, exposing herself even more to him.

He smiled at her as he slipped his hands under her ass again and lifted her to his mouth. "This is how I like you. Your pretty pink folds open and ready for me." He dragged his tongue through her and looked up again. "Ready to be taken hard by my cock."

Her pussy twitched, and fire coiled in her belly. Usually dirty talk made her feel embarrassed and awkward, but Torven's words only stoked her passion and made her feel more desirable and more beautiful.

Trista let her eyes close, fisting her hands by her side as he kissed the inside of her thighs before parting her with his tongue. She was already so close to the edge again that she nearly broke apart when he started lapping her. He moved up to her clit and circled it like she'd done, increasing his speed when she arched into him. He groaned and the vibrations of his mouth shot through her.

"I'm going to come on your tongue," she managed to say, grasping the back of his head as he sucked her clit and shattered her into pieces.

Trista bucked against him, but he held her legs tightly, licking her as she came, and making the ripples of pleasure tear through her again and again. She finally went boneless, her hands releasing their grip on his hair.

"So sweet," he murmured from between her legs. "Tasting your juices and licking your little nub has made my cock like steel."

"Show me," she said. She'd never been so bold as to give orders to a guy, but she liked the way it felt. "I want to see that hard cock."

He lifted one eyebrow and straightened up so that his cock emerged from the water. Thick and long, it stood out from his body as water dripped off. Torven fisted it.

Trista loved that she'd made him so hard, and she loved the way he looked at her as if he wanted to devour every inch of her. It made her feel powerful and sexy.

"I thought you promised to fuck me hard," she said, dragging a finger through her own wet folds.

He growled and took one leg in each hand. "Watch me claim you, mate."

Her breath hitched as his crown parted her. She already felt stretched, and he was barely inside her. Before she could ask him to go slow, he drove into her.

Trista gasped as he impaled her on his cock, holding himself deep inside.

"So tight." His words came out jerky and hard. "Am I hurting you, *cinnara*?"

She felt full in a way she never had before, but it didn't hurt. "Feels good."

He thrust in again, then sat back and looked at where they were joined. “Love seeing you stretched around my cock.” He stroked in again. “So tight and pink and perfect.”

At that moment, she believed she was perfect. His hands clamped down on her hips, and he powered into her again and again with a fierce rhythm. As he began to pulse into her, he dropped his mouth to hers and swallowed both of their screams.

Trista wrapped her legs around his waist, holding him inside her. She could feel his heart hammering in his chest as he sank on top of her, bracing his arms on the rock floor to keep from crushing her. The feel of him snug inside her and the sound of his heartbeat echoing through her own chest was something she never wanted to end.

CHAPTER NINETEEN

Torven rolled over on to the stone floor, panting heavily. He could hear Trista's rapid breathing next to him, and he twisted his head to look at her.

She lay sprawled out, with her feet dangling in the water and her bare skin flushed. The pink flesh around her nipples was still pebbled, and his breath caught just looking at her lush body.

Glancing over at him, Trista gave a dazed smile. She sidled up closer to him, hooking one of her legs around his. Smiling back, he used one arm to pull her closer.

Her eyes drifted to his cock, which had already begun to rise. She playfully swatted his chest. "Oh, no you don't."

"What?" He assumed his most innocent voice. "I thought you said you liked it hard."

The blush on her cheeks deepened. "That's not playing fair. Besides, I think we both need a second to recover."

"You want a break?"

Her eyebrows popped up. "Don't you need one?"

He shook his head as he stroked one hand down her back until he reached the cleft between her ass cheeks. "Why would I need to stop?"

Trista laughed. "So I guess that's one more way you aren't like human men."

Torven swept a strand of damp hair off her forehead and planted a kiss on the top of her head. "Are there many differences?"

"A few." Trista said, letting her eyes wander lower. She pushed herself up and scooted toward the edge of the pool, then let herself drop into the water, sinking up to her neck. "This feels so good. Want to join me?"

Even though his legs still twitched, Torven scooted himself to the pool and slipped in. The steaming water did feel good as he submerged his entire body and then came up and floated on his back with his hands laced behind his head. He knew he should feel guilty for claiming her when he had no right to her, but he didn't. He actually felt better than he had in a long time. Even the worry over being a fugitive and being chased by the Kronock seemed far away, as they relaxed in the warm, natural-spring pool.

He looked up at the ceiling of the cave, the blue glow of the walls bouncing off the water and reflecting undulating waves of light. It was as if they'd slipped into another world when they'd discovered the underground cavern, one he never would have expected given the unforgiving terrain outside. Torven breathed in the steamy air, his nose having become used to the odd smell. Had anyone ever discovered this place before, or was it theirs alone?

The only sound was that of the water lapping the sides of the rock, and it was easy to imagine they were out of reach of everyone. Few knew they were even on the planet, Torven thought, and those who did had no clue about the underground paradise. What if they stayed there? He'd never have to answer for crimes he didn't commit, and he'd never have to risk losing her.

He rolled over in the water and swam a few strokes toward Trista. Now more than ever, he couldn't imagine giving her up. Anger surged through him at the thought. She was his mate. He knew in his gut she had always been meant for him, and she would always be his. No matter what.

He wrapped his arms around her, pulling her tightly to his chest. Feeling her softness pressed against him gave him a sense of comfort. She belonged with him.

"You can swim," Trista said, dropping her head back to look up at him. "I didn't think all Drexians could. Mandy almost drowned Dorn by pushing him into the water outside her fantasy suite."

"So, you aren't the only human female to attempt to kill her mate," Torven said as he turned his head to avoid Trista splashing water at him.

"Maybe if you all weren't such stubborn alpha males," Trista said, but her voice was playful.

"When I first graduated from the Drexian military academy, I was stationed on a planet that was mostly water," Torven said. "Learning to swim was necessary to survive."

"So do any Drexians *not* become warriors?" Trista asked.

"The few females we had rarely went to the Academy. But all Drexian males become warriors—for a time, at least. Fighting and defending are in our blood."

"So if everyone's in the military, who builds things, or repairs things, or invents things?"

"Some Drexians serve on High Command or become scientists or engineers after military service, but all the aliens whose planets we've saved from being invaded lend us their talents. Like the Vexling you were standing with on the space station. Vexlings are known as great linguists and diplomats. We saved the planet Vex from the Kronock many years ago, and now some of their people work for us."

Trista took a step back. "They aren't slaves, are they?"

Torven frowned. "Of course not. Drexians would never enslave. We have an equal exchange of labor. Our warriors are stationed on their planet, and some of their people choose to work for us. And get compensated."

"I didn't know if it was like the deal with Earth, where you take Vexlings without their permission."

Torven flinched. "We have permission from Earth."

"The government bigwigs maybe, but not the women who get snatched," Trista said, not meeting his eyes.

"That was the choice of your planet. We would have preferred to be open about the exchange, as we have been with other worlds."

"I'll bet if women on Earth knew there were a bunch of hot aliens looking for brides, you'd have them fighting to come to the Boat."

Torven paused before asking his question, not sure if he wanted to hear the answer. "Would you have been one of them?"

She hesitated. "Honestly, I don't know. The thought of leaving Earth, or even Iowa, might have freaked me out. But maybe not as much as just ending up on the station out of the blue, and trying to come to terms with the whole deal. I was pretty upset for a while."

He stroked a hand down her back. "Are you still upset?"

She smirked up at him. "You mean, am I freaked out by being kidnapped again, crashing on an ice planet, being almost eaten by an alien albino alligator, and running for my life from the Kronock? Why would that freak me out?"

"I am sorry to have put you in danger," he said.

She ran a hand down his chest and stomach, letting her fingers bump along the defined ridges. "You know the weird thing? As much danger as we've been in, and are probably still in, I don't feel unsafe with you. You look like you should be a bad guy, but you aren't."

Her touch made his cock stir. He watched as she traced the tip of her finger around his crown. "I will do anything to keep you safe," he said, his voice cracking. "You are my mate, my *cinnara*, my little grease monkey."

She made a face and splashed him before sliding her hand up the length of his cock. "I've never been able to be so free with a guy. I'd usually be embarrassed."

"There is no reason to be embarrassed by pleasuring your mate." Torven moved a hand around from her back and cupped one of her plump breasts, thumbing her nipple and watching it become a tight point. He didn't like thinking of her with any other males, but he pushed aside his jealousy. "There are many more ways I intend to have you, and I promise you will enjoy them all."

She made a soft sound of pleasure in the back of her throat, but dipped her body below the surface of the water. "Not so fast. It's my turn to play." She took his stiff cock in one hand underwater.

He hardened even more in her hand. When she traced her top lip with her tongue, Torven's eyes nearly rolled up into his head.

"Since I don't have gills," she said, "I need you to stand for me."

He obeyed her, rising to his feet and letting the water sluice off his body.

She stayed kneeling in the pool, his cock now at eye level. Wetting her bottom lip, she winked at him. "So lickable."

He watched as she took the head of his cock between her lips, closing his eyes as the feeling of her hot, wet mouth overwhelmed him. She sucked him hard, and he let out a contented moan.

Opening his eyes, he looked down as she slid his length in and out of her mouth. He almost exploded into her at the sight of her pink lips stretched around his thick crown. She pulled back and traced the tip of her tongue around the hard ridge and then down the thick vein that ran underneath. Wrapping her fingers tight around his girth, she pulled him into her mouth again.

He gritted his teeth. Trista had almost his entire length in her mouth. Watching her made it hard not to burst, but he held back and put his hands on the back of her head. She pumped the base of his cock with one hand as she moved her mouth, and the combination made him ball his hands into her wet hair. Being inside her mouth reminded him of being inside her tight heat, and his cock jerked.

"Show me how fast or slow you want it," Trista said, looking up at him. "Guide me."

He grunted in agreement as he used the hands on the back of her head to pull her closer. He moved her in a steady rhythm, the view of her sucking down his cock almost mesmerizing. "Can't believe you're taking so much of me."

Her pace became quicker and his breath jagged. When she moaned, it vibrated down the length of his shaft.

"I can't hold back any longer," he said, his words rough and jerky.

She reached around with one hand, grabbing his ass and pulling him deeper, his cock bumping up against the back of her throat. It was too much for him to handle, and he threw back his head and roared as he pulsed into her mouth.

Trista held him inside her as she swallowed, then she sat back. "That was fun."

Torven wasn't sure what had happened to the hesitant female he'd taken from the station, but this feisty, insatiable version was even better than he could have imagined.

CHAPTER TWENTY

"This isn't pad-whatever, is it?" Trista asked, as Torven handed her one of the foil food pouches from his pack. She didn't know how long they'd been down in the cavern, but they'd already gone through half of the food in her bag. At least twenty-four hours, she'd guess, although there was no way to tell underground. And they'd been too busy getting their fill of each other to notice the passage of time.

He laughed. "No, although many Drexians love padwump rind."

Trista sat cross-legged next to him with her environmental suit halfway on and the sleeves tied around her waist to keep it from slipping down. She wore her black T-shirt, the fabric sticking to her skin. The air was too steamy for them to dry completely, but she wasn't complaining. She'd rather be hot and humid than freezing her ass off outside.

She tore open the shiny pouch, and tentatively sniffed the contents. It didn't have a distinct smell, unlike the salty tang of the padwump rind. She hoped that was a good sign. She'd found most of the packaged food to be palatable so far, although she would have killed for a decent hamburger.

Torven started to say something, but she held up a hand. "Don't tell me what it is. I'm too hungry to care anymore, but I'd rather not know if I'm eating eye of newt."

He raised an eyebrow and mouthed the words "eye of newt" to himself, but remained quiet as they ate.

The thin, flat strips were a bit chewy with a bland taste, but Trista was fine with that. She thought back to the food on the station and groaned out loud.

"You like it?" Torven asked.

"Sorry about that. I was thinking about the food on the Boat."

"I have heard they have Gatazoid chefs," Torven said. "Gatazoids are known throughout the galaxy as being great artisans. I imagine the food is quite delicious."

"I don't know who the chefs are," Trista said. "But they make a mean steak."

Torven wrinkled his brow. "A mean steak? The steak is unkind?"

Trista giggled. "It's an expression. It just means that it's really good."

Torven swallowed a bite of what he was eating. "I hope I get the chance to sample this mean steak one day."

Trista's pulse fluttered. "Me too. I want to show you our fantasy suite."

"Tell me about it." Torven leaned closer to her and rested his elbows on his knees.

Normally, Trista would feel nervous with his face only inches from hers, and the body heat radiating off his bare chest. He'd been too warm to put his T-shirt back on, and wore only his snug boxer briefs. Up until recently, being that close to a mostly naked guy with huge, tattooed arms would have sent off warning bells in her head. Instead of feeling jittery, though, Trista's own body hummed with excitement.

Her mind flashed back to lying sprawled out on the stone floor while he licked her and of the subsequent places around the cavern he'd taken her since then—up against the stone wall, sitting on one of the rounder rock formations, in the pool at least three more times

—and her body warmed in response. Nope. Scared was definitely not what she felt when she was with him.

Well," she said. "It's supposed to be on a Greek island, so it's all white with a private pool that looks out over the cliff to the ocean. And of course since it's a hologram, I get both sunsets and sunrises from the balcony."

"Does it look like that place on Earth?"

"I've never been there, but it looks like the pictures. From what I've heard, all of the fantasy suites are based off places on Earth. Really exotic places that I've never seen."

Torven reached for one of the metal canisters of water. "I am eager to stay in this place with you."

Trista took the water that he offered her, swallowing a cool gulp. "You've never been to the Boat before?"

He shook his head. "Aside from when we met, no. There is no reason to go, unless we are matched with a tribute bride, and that can often take a long time. I have heard many talk about it, though."

"I'm guessing it's different from your other space stations."

"We do not have other stations," Torven said. "We have many battleships, however, and most warriors get assigned to these. We also have outposts on planets we protect."

"What about your home planet?" Trista asked. Despite living on their station, she realized she didn't know that much about the Drexian race, aside from how hot they were.

"The Drexian home world?" Torven's face clouded. "It was once beautiful, but years of war destroyed it. Now, only the elders remain. That is why we fight so hard to maintain peace in the galaxy. Drexian warriors spend our lives living in space, defending those who cannot defend themselves."

Trista swallowed a mouthful of the dried food. "You live your entire lives on spaceships?"

He shrugged. "We do not think of it like that. Besides, our battleships are large, so it does not feel cramped."

"Like the Boat, where you can forget you're floating in space?"

He crumpled up his empty foil packet. "Yes, although we do not have holographic suites. I look forward to experiencing that with you."

Trista shifted where she sat. She wanted that, too, but it felt like a faraway dream. "Do you think that will actually happen? Do you think we'll actually get to be together? Officially, I mean."

"I have faith that my friends will find the real traitor and prove me innocent," Torven said. "You do believe I'm innocent, don't you?"

"Of course. I've known a lot of bad guys in my life, and you're not like any of them."

Torven's intent gaze made her look down and shift her position on the hard rock floor. She'd probably said too much. No guy likes to think about his girl having a past.

"These bad guys hurt you." It was a statement, not a question.

Trista didn't look up but nodded. "Yeah, but that's in the past. It has nothing to do with you."

Torven rested one large hand on her knee. "If we were not stranded on a barren planet, I would want to fly down to Earth and punish these men for hurting you."

Trista couldn't help but smile and looked up to meet his eyes. "Thanks, I think. Speaking of being stuck on this ice heap, what's your plan for escaping the Kronock?"

"If they knew where we were, we would already in be custody. Or dead. I suspect this mountain has many tunnels, and possibly many more underground springs. It could take a very long time, if they have to search every one of them."

"So we hide out down here?" Trista glanced around the blue glow of the cavern, and breathed in the moist air. She guessed there were worse places to hang out, but she didn't really want to spend the rest of her life there. Not to mention the fact that they would run out of rations before too long.

"I should go to the surface and see if any other vessels have arrived," Torven said.

"Whoa. I thought the plan was to hide in here."

"You will stay here," he said. "I will go to the top to check and then return."

"No way, José," Trista said. "I'm not letting you leave me down here. What if you don't come back? What if they grab you at the surface? What if I try to get out and go into the wrong corridor? If you're going up to the surface, I'm going with you."

Torven frowned. "Are all human females as difficult as you?"

"I'm not difficult," Trista said. "I told you. I just don't like being bossed around."

"I cannot imagine anyone being successful at bossing you around," Torven muttered under his breath.

"You didn't mind me being bossy earlier," she reminded him.

"When you milked my cock with your mouth?" He said, dropping his voice low. "No, I did not mind that at all."

Even though she knew they were alone, his words made her face flame. She gaped at him. "Torven!"

He set down his packet of food and tugged her onto his lap. "You wish to call my name out again?"

"I thought we were going to the surface," she said, her protests weak as he kissed her neck.

"Soon," he said. "First things, first."

CHAPTER TWENTY-ONE

Torven helped Trista pull her environmental suit up over her clothes, the blue glow of the cavern making the suit shimmer an iridescent blue. She looked up at him, her cheeks pink from the warm air.

He wanted to tear the suit off her, not zip it up, but he also knew they should check the surface of the planet. As much as he wanted to stay below with her forever, safe in a place where no one could pass judgment on him or separate them, he knew it was not possible. He needed to get her off the planet and to safety before the Kronock found them. The last thing he wanted was for help to arrive and for him to miss it because they were down below. Torven also knew he should be restraining himself around her.

Unless Dorn and Dakar had been able to pull off a miracle and clear his name already, he was still a criminal in the eyes of the Drexian High Command. And that meant he wasn't entitled to a tribute bride. As much as he knew in his heart that Trista was meant for him, he doubted others would see it that way. If he was convicted, Trista would be matched with another Drexian warrior. What they'd done in the warm springs beneath the surface of the planet would not matter to anyone. His stomach clenched as he imagined his mate with another. He could not let that happen.

"I think that's tight enough," Trista said, sucking in as he cinched the waist of her suit so it wouldn't sag.

"Sorry." He realized he was so lost in his thoughts he'd forgotten to stop tightening. Torven let go and stepped away.

Trista breathed out in relief. "You seemed far away just then."

"Just thinking of what might await us up there," he said.

She nodded and cast a glance around the cavern. "It's not too late to change our minds. I've definitely seen worse apartments in my life."

Torven thought about their stolen hours together in the cavern and how many times she'd screamed his name. It wasn't hard to imagine hiding out with Trista for weeks, but he knew it wasn't how either of them wanted to spend the rest of their lives. Even if they did manage to find enough food on the planet to survive, he'd always be considered an outlaw. He shook his head. He did not want his family to have to say his name with shame.

"We will return," he said, trying to sound more confident than he felt.

She hoisted her pack over one arm. "I guess we'd better do this before I lose my nerve."

"You are nervous about going to the surface again because it is cold?"

"No." She bit her lower lip. "It's the dark of the tunnels I don't like. We have no idea how many there are under the mountain or if they all connect to the surface. We ended up down here by taking a fork we didn't even notice the first time. What if we accidentally take another fork, and end up wandering forever in the dark?"

He noticed her hand shake, and pulled her close. "I will not let that happen."

She sank into his arms. "I also don't welcome the idea of being taken captive by the Kronock. Bridget told me what happened to her when she was kidnapped by them, and I do not want to be stripped naked and strapped to a table."

"Bridget?"

"Another tribute bride. The enemy took her. From what she said, they aren't nice guys."

Torven stiffened at the thought of the Kronock taking his mate and binding her to a table. He would kill them all before he'd let that happen. Or he would die trying.

"I will always keep you safe," he said, as he raised her face to his and kissed her gently. "Are you sure you won't stay here?"

"Who would keep you safe?" she teased.

He kissed her again, this time, going deeper. Frissons of pleasure shot all the way to his fingertips, and he pulled back before the tingling sensation gave way to a pulsating desire that was hard to resist. "We should go."

Torven gave a final look at the luminous blue cavern with its steamy pool and felt a pang of regret. It was hard to leave when he didn't know what would be waiting for them above, but he swallowed his fear. He pulled the blaster from his belt and took her hand in his as they entered the tunnel they'd come from. After a few steps, the darkness swallowed them, and the only sounds were their echoing footsteps and heavy breathing as they trudged uphill.

Torven walked with one elbow bowed out and brushing the wall so he would not accidentally go off course and inadvertently enter another tunnel. The walk was steep, and soon Trista was sucking in air.

"Are you okay?" he asked.

"Peachy," she said. "It reminds me why I despise cardio."

He wasn't sure what she meant, but she sounded fine. He assumed "peachy" was an Earth word that meant she was okay.

They continued to trudge upward, and Torven began to worry they were no longer in the tunnel that would reach the exit. Had it taken so long to reach the natural springs below? He couldn't remember, but he thought they should be nearing the top.

"How much longer?" Trista asked between gasps.

"Almost there," Torven said, although he was not sure himself. At what point did he admit they were lost and turn around? Could they even find the cavern again, or was Trista right? Was it possible they could wander in the subterranean tunnels without ever finding an escape?

Torven pushed the thought out of his mind, along with the urge to yell. The darkness felt heavy—as if it was enveloping him—and he imagined the air getting thinner as he tried to suck in deep breaths. He needed to stay calm for Trista, he told himself, even as he wanted nothing more than to claw at his own throat.

"There," Trista tugged on his hand. "Isn't that light?"

Torven squinted into the blackness. She was right. The faintest glow was coming from somewhere in front of them. He walked faster and the glow became daylight, and then he had to shield his eyes from the glare of white outside the mouth of the tunnel.

He stepped out onto the icy ground and blinked, temporarily blinded by the ice and snow. The air, which had gotten progressively cooler as they'd walked up the tunnel, was bracing once they were out in the open. He instantly missed the warmth and seclusion of the underground springs.

Torven turned to Trista, relieved to have made it out safely, and pulled her into an embrace, lifting her feet from the ground.

"We did it," she said, letting out a long sigh. "I've never been so happy to see miles of snow and ice before."

He stepped back from her and looked down at her face. He leaned in for a kiss, but his breath caught when he saw her expression change. Her eyes were wide, and her mouth open as she stared past him.

Torven swung around, but all he could see was the blaster pointing at his face.

CHAPTER TWENTY-TWO

"Dak?" Torven nearly fell to his knees when he realized his best friend was on the other end of the blaster.

"Gods, Torven." Dakar lowered the blaster and let out a loud sigh. "Is that really you?"

Torven was so relieved to see his friend and not be shot by a Kronock that he pulled Dakar into a hug, thumping the Drexian hard on the back, then held him at arm's length.

His Inferno Force crewmate wore an environmental suit like the one they had on, although his did not look so weathered as it reflected the white snow and ice. He wore the hood flipped back and his brown hair was tied up in a messy bun. Torven noted the stubble on his cheeks and the dark circles under his eyes. "You don't look so good, my friend."

Dakar cocked an eyebrow. "Tearing around the galaxy looking for my best friend and trying to save his ass from being executed has taken it out of me." He gave Torven the once-over. "You look surprisingly well for a fugitive."

Torven glanced down as Trista cleared her throat behind him. "I haven't been alone. This is Trista." His eyes went to his mate. "This is Dakar, a member of Inferno Force and my closest friend."

Dakar gave her a small bow. "An honor to meet you." He pivoted to face Torven again. "I heard you kidnapped a bride from the station, but I couldn't believe it at first."

"It's true," Torven said. "It was the only way to get off the station."

"It does not make you look good. The High Command is insisting an innocent Drexian would not run."

Torven tried to control his anger. "They would if they were being set up. You know I'm incapable of committing treason."

"You do not have to convince me. I know you are no traitor." He rubbed a hand across his forehead. "But you can imagine how they are making this look. A violent criminal drags a tribute bride off the station."

"He didn't drag me," Trista said, her own voice brimming with irritation. "And I shot him once we were on the shuttle."

The corners of Dakar's mouth twitched up, and he glanced at Torven. "She got the drop on you?" His eyes shifted back to Trista. "I think I like you already."

"My tribute bride has tried to kill me more than once," Torven said, avoiding the look he knew she was shooting him.

"I told you I was not trying to kill you the last time," she said. "I was saving you."

Torven rubbed the back of his head. "It still left a bruise."

Dakar stared between the two. "Your tribute bride? Are you telling me this is the female you were matched with?"

"Yes," Torven said. "Did you not know this?"

Dakar shook his head and his topknot bobbled. "I did not stop for long at the station. I only met with Dorn briefly, and I guess he did not think that information was relevant."

Torven stepped closer. "What has Dorn discovered?"

Dakar glanced back over his shoulder. "There is too much to tell you out here. We should get out of sight. These hills are crawling with Kronock."

Torven nodded and his eyes darted around the craggy rock face.

"Of course, you are right. We should go below the surface again where they won't find us."

Dakar peered at the dark mouth of the tunnel. "Is this why I haven't been able to get a lock on your location for hours? You're under miles of bedrock? Is that why the tribute's tracker isn't showing up on sensors?"

"I cut that out of her as soon as we left the station," Torven said, as Dakar's eyes grew large.

"You cut...?"

"Your friend is a brute," Trista told him, with a grin.

Dakar returned her smile with a dazzling one of his own, reminding Torven of his friend's ease with females. "That I know well."

Torven cleared his throat and jerked a head toward the tunnel. "Enough talking out here in the open. Come. You'll see."

Trista reached a hand for his, but he did not take it. He did not want Dakar to become even more suspicious than he already was. Torven had noticed the way Dakar was watching them, as if he couldn't quite decide what was actually going on.

If Dakar knew what had happened between them, he would know that Torven had crossed a line. It was one thing to kidnap a tribute bride, it was quite another to claim her while being on the run and living as a fugitive.

Torven's heart raced as he thought about how he'd taken her—in the hot spring, up against the rock wall, with her balancing on a boulder. No, Dakar would not understand their connection. He would only think that Torven had taken advantage of a human female who might never be his. And he would be right. If Torven was never vindicated, he would never have a legitimate claim to Trista. His stomach twisted at the thought, but he didn't look at his mate.

"I will lead the way," he said, "but it is dark, so be careful."

Dakar took a metal cylinder off his belt and clicked it once. A light shone from the end. "Would this help?"

Torven let out a relieved laugh as he took the light. "Most of my tools went down with the shuttle."

"When you say, 'went down . . . ?'" Dakar said.

Torven entered the tunnel and Trista fell in step behind him. "Into the icy lake we thought was a valley."

Dakar looked back at the frozen terrain before following. "Do you think you could have found a less hospitable planet, my friend?"

"The next time I crash land on a planet, I will make sure it meets your standards, Dak."

The two crewmates traded barbs back and forth as they descended beneath the mountain, but Torven was very aware of Trista's silence. He hadn't been able to explain why he couldn't show affection for her around his friend, and he doubted she understood his sudden coolness. He'd gone from having his cock buried inside her to avoiding her touch. His face burned with shame as he thought of how this must seem to her.

He stole a glance behind him, but her face was unreadable in the warm glow of the light bouncing off the curved rock walls. He and Dakar had to walk slightly bent as the tunnel dropped, and he saw his friend's topknot scraping against the roof as he followed along behind Trista.

The air slowly became warmer and wetter, a sure sign they were on the right path and would soon be in the cavern with the hot springs.

"Is there an end to this journey?" Dak asked. "Not that I do not prefer it to the frigid surface and avoiding our enemy."

Torven spotted the blue glow ahead. "We are almost there."

Trista breathed heavily behind him, and he realized how quickly he'd been walking. Dakar had easily kept up, since he also had long legs and a wide stride, but Trista must have been nearly jogging to keep pace with them. As he exited the tunnel and entered the cavern, he waited for her. "I am sorry if I went too fast."

She waved his comment away with a flick of her hand. "I'm fine. You don't need to worry about me."

Her face was blank. She didn't look like she was upset, but there was no warmth in her voice.

"I did not expect this," Dak said, as he walked around the massive stalactites embedded with millions of glowing blue flecks. He tilted his head back to take in the rock formations that looked as if blobs of rock had been poured from above and suddenly hardened. He walked over to the steaming spring pool and dipped his hand in. "I take it the Kronock have no idea this exists."

"Not as far as we know," Torven said, glancing at Trista who was peeling off her environmental suit. "I doubt they had any interest in this planet before we arrived."

"Not surprising." Dakar sat down and leaned his back against one of the wider stalagmites. "How soon did they turn up after you crashed?"

"They weren't chasing us, if that's what you're asking." Torven sat across from his friend and tried not to cast worried glances at Trista, who was now dangling her feet in the pool. "We lost one engine and landed the shuttle to see if we could make repairs, but there wasn't a Kronock on our tail."

"Is that when the shuttle went into the lake?" his friend asked.

"First, we were chased by some kind of amphibious monster," Torven said. "Then the shuttle went into the lake."

Dakar raised an eyebrow. "You're really selling this place."

"Well, I hope we don't have to stay here. Please tell me Dorn has found something that proves I'm innocent."

Dakar leaned forward, resting his elbows on his knees. "Both he and his brother, Kax, who's in military intelligence, are working on it. From what he told me, they've been suspicious of someone in the High Command for a while now. There were some issues with sabotage recently, and another warrior was blamed until they realized he'd been set up."

Torven slapped his hand against the hard rock floor. "What kind of Drexian would do such a thing?"

"One who has no problem working with the enemy," Dakar said. "They must be getting something out of it, to go to such lengths."

Torven shook his head. "There is nothing worth sacrificing your honor."

"Agreed." Dakar's face was solemn. "But whoever is doing this is powerful enough to cover their tracks, so we must be careful."

Torven calmed his breathing. "Did Dorn have any idea how long their investigation would take?"

"No, although he did mention doing something to draw out the traitor. I do not think you will need to be on the run for much longer."

"Good," Trista said, from where she sat. "I've had about enough of being a hostage."

Torven couldn't help feeling the sting of her words. If he hadn't been certain if she was upset before, he was now.

CHAPTER
TWENTY-THREE

Trista scissored her feet in the warm water and breathed in the faint sulphur smell. A bit of water splashed up onto her rolled-up jeans as she glanced over her shoulder.

Not long ago, she'd been in that same water with her legs wrapped around Torven's waist. Now, he sat huddled with his friend, discussing strategy for proving his innocence, while she sat alone. She kicked her legs faster, sending droplets of water flying.

It was clear he didn't want his friend to know they'd been together. As soon as Dakar showed up, Torven had cooled off toward her. Was he embarrassed that he'd slept with her? Her eyes stung with tears she refused to let drop. She looked up at the iridescent-blue ceiling of the cavern, blinking hard.

He wouldn't be the first guy who'd ignored her, or tried to pretend they weren't together, but she'd really thought he was different. She'd felt a connection with him she'd never experienced before. At least, she thought she had.

She peeked over her shoulder to where the two Drexians sat, deep in conversation. Even seeing his broad back and dark tattoos swirling below the sleeve of his shirt made her pulse flutter. Trista jerked her gaze away. How could she have been stupid enough to trust him?

He'd kidnapped her, for fuck's sake. Shouldn't that have told her everything she needed to know? Why did she convince herself that this guy was different? That he wasn't really bad, even though everyone else thought he was?

"So much for not getting mixed up with bad boys anymore," she muttered to herself.

A little voice in the back of her head reminded her that she didn't think he was guilty, and neither did his friends. Maybe he wasn't a traitor, but that didn't mean he hadn't used her. Did he even intend to go through with the wedding ceremony, or had he gotten what he'd wanted from her? There was no guarantee he'd ever be proven innocent and get to return to his people, much less come to live with her on the Boat.

Trista looked around the cave as the eerie light bounced off the water and reflected undulating wave patterns on the huge stalactites. Was she willing to stay with him, even if they could never be officially bonded?

Her face flamed as she thought back to how she felt when he was inside her. It had been amazing, but better than that, it had felt right. As if they'd been made for each other. Trista squeezed her legs together at the memory. She was still sore from him, but she definitely wanted more. But how was that any different than her exboyfriends back home that could never make a commitment? Hadn't she convinced herself of the same thing back then? That good sex was enough to make up for being ignored?

"Fuck that shit," she whispered.

"Trista?"

Torven's voice made her spin her head around and realize she'd spoken louder than she'd intended.

His brows pressed together to form a crease between his eyes. She thought she read regret in his expression, but she was probably imagining it.

"Nothing," she said, turning back to the water. "Just talking to myself."

She heard him get up and walk to her. "Dakar has food in his pack. Better than our rations."

She didn't want to look at him, but she had to admit she was hungry. Her stomach growled. She wasn't sure the freeze-dried food in the foil packets counted as a decent meal, and she found herself longing for real food.

"Not dehydrated rations?" she asked, glancing up at Torven.

He grinned at her and held out a hand to pull her up. "No, although I do not think you gave those a fair try. Padwump rind is an acquired taste."

Trista didn't smile back, and didn't take his hand. If he wanted to play it cool, two could play at that game.

"Has my friend been serving you padwump rind?" Dakar asked, shaking his head and shooting Torven a look. "This is not how to impress a guest."

Trista sat next to Dakar and smiled at him. She liked his messy man bun and scruff, and couldn't help staring at his vivid-teal eyes. Drexian eyes came in more colors than she'd ever imagined, and it was hard not to feel pulled in by them.

"I didn't know I was a guest," she said. "I think captive is a better word."

Dakar's eyebrows lifted, and his eyes flicked over her head. Torven grunted behind her before settling himself on her other side. He clearly didn't like her comment, but he didn't say anything.

"Well, you are a guest," Dakar said, giving her a dazzling smile. "At least now."

She returned his smile. Even though she liked the thought of making Torven squirm, she also genuinely liked his friend. He seemed easygoing instead of intense, and had no problem poking fun at Torven.

Dakar unwrapped a bundle and held it out to her. "I'm told these are delicacies on Earth."

Trista stifled a laugh as she peered down at the rings of dough. "Bagels? I don't know if I'd call them a delicacy, but I've never been as happy to see one in my life."

She bit into a bagel and closed her eyes as she chewed. It wasn't exactly what she'd pick for a last meal, but after dehydrated rations, it tasted heavenly.

"I have more of these I will leave with you," Dakar said. "I ransacked the kitchens on the Boat when I stopped there."

Trista swallowed. "Wait. You're leaving?"

Dakar didn't meet her eyes. "If I disappear for too long, they might suspect I've located Torven. I don't want to inadvertently give away his location until I'm sure Dorn has the information needed to clear his name."

"After Dak rests, he will leave us and try to draw the Kronock away from the planet," Torven said. "That will buy us more time."

"Us?" Trista asked, still not turning to face him. "Why do I have to stay here?"

Dakar and Torven were silent but she knew they exchanged a look over her head. She finally twisted so she could see Torven.

"You don't need me anymore, right?" Her eyes narrowed at him. "I mean, you already got what you wanted from me."

His mouth opened, and a flush of red began to climb his neck, but he didn't speak.

"You needed to use me to get off the station," she continued. "You got off. You escaped. You don't need me anymore. I'm sure I'm just a liability to you now."

"You are not a liability." His voice was a low growl. "You are my..."

She leveled her gaze at him. "Your what, Torven?"

"Maybe she should leave," Dakar said. "Releasing her could help your case when this finally gets resolved. I can take her back with me, and she can explain that you didn't mistreat her and—"

"No!" Torven's booming voice echoed off the cavern's walls.

"Torven?" Dakar eyed his friend warily.

"She does not leave," Torven said, his voice shaking. "I need her for leverage."

"Leverage?" Dakar shook his head. "It is true the Drexians won't do anything to risk her, but can you say the same of the Kronock? What if you're both captured by our enemy? Do you really want her falling into their hands?"

Torven leapt to his feet and strode across the cavern. "I will not let that happen. I will keep her safe."

"So, I can't leave?" Trista jumped up and spun around to face Torven.

His hands were in tight fists by his side. "You want to leave?"

She hesitated, thinking about their limbs entwined in the water and the feel of his big arms around her. Then she thought of him pulling his hand away from hers and was reminded of every guy who'd pretended to care for her then ignored her as soon as his friends came around. "Do I want to get off this ice planet and go back to my home on the Boat where I have people who actually care about me? Hell, yeah, I do."

He took a step back as if he'd been slapped. His eyes flared with anger as he glared back at her. "I cannot let you go. I need you."

"So much for not being a hostage." She turned away from him and sank back down next to Dakar, keeping her head down so he wouldn't see the tears in her eyes.

"Torven, why don't—?" Dakar began, his tone calm.

"No more discussion," Torven snapped. "She cannot leave with you."

Dakar sighed.

"You should get some rest, if you plan to leave in the morning, Dak," Torven said, his voice gruff. He came up behind Trista and rested a hand on her shoulder. "You should also sleep."

She jerked her shoulder out of his grasp. "Get away from me."

She heard his sharp intake of breath, then his heavy footsteps as he stormed to the far side of the cavern.

Dakar handed the remaining bagels to Trista without a word.

She looked down at them through a haze of angry tears. She'd thought Torven was different, but he wanted to control her just like all the rest of them had.

She swiped away hot tears and folded up the packet of bagels. She'd see about that.

CHAPTER TWENTY-FOUR

Torven woke up and rolled over on the hard, rock floor. His neck ached as he sat up and squinted through the dim blue glow of the cavern. Although he preferred the steamy air to the sub-zero temperatures outside, he had a hard time sleeping when he was hot, and he'd stripped down to his pants during the night. He groaned as his cock stiffened, and he tried to ignore it.

The dreams he'd had about Trista all night hadn't helped. He'd rolled over many times, reaching for her soft body, to find nothing but scratchy rock beneath him. All he wanted was to prove his innocence so he could return to the Boat and wake up every morning beside her.

He hadn't slept near his mate, even though he'd wanted to, and now his eyes scoured the cavern for her. When he'd gone to sleep, she'd been curled up against the far wall. Now she was no longer there. He reached for his black shirt and pulled it on over his head. Jumping up, he walked quickly around the various rock formations protruding from the ground in case she was behind one of them. Nothing. Another scan of the cavern told him her pack was also missing. His stomach became a hard knot.

"Dak, wake up." He shook his sleeping friend by the shoulder.

Dakar blinked up at him and rubbed his eyes. "What? You interrupted my dream. I was on one of the pleasure planets with a very alluring Xendrian."

"Trista is gone," Torven said, pacing as his friend stood.

"Trista?" Dakar looked around as he rubbed his eyes. "Are you sure?"

Torven threw his arms out wide. "Of course I'm sure. This isn't a huge cavern, and I've searched all of it. She isn't here. She left sometime while we were sleeping."

Dakar scratched at the scruff on his chin. "Well, she didn't seem too happy when you told her she couldn't leave."

Torven frowned and made a low noise in the back of his throat. "Why would she want to leave? It's dangerous out there. I already saved her from dying once." He dragged a hand through his hair. "What was she thinking?"

"She clearly wanted to get away. Are you sure you didn't terrify her?" Dakar's hair was loose, and he twisted it up into a topknot as he spoke.

Torven gave an abrupt shake of his head. "Everything was fine until last night. I thought she..."

Dakar studied his friend's reaction. "What is it you aren't telling me, friend?"

"*Grek.*" Torven mumbled the curse, strode across the cavern, and snatched his pack from the floor. "I made a mistake."

"What kind of mistake?"

Torven let out a long breath but didn't meet his friend's eyes." I know it was wrong and I should've waited, but we were matched before I was falsely accused. She's my mate, Dak. I feel it. We are meant to be together."

A look of understanding crossed Dakar's face. "So you...?"

"Yes," Torven shouted, and then dropped his voice. "I claimed her."

Dakar sighed. "That explains why she was so upset with you yesterday."

"So, you could tell...?" Torven asked as he pulled on his environmental suit, the fabric shimmering blue from the glowing light.

"I could tell there was something going on, but you did not behave like a mated couple," Dakar said. "She definitely didn't seem to like you."

Torven stared at the ground. "I did not want you to know my dishonor. I know it was wrong to claim her when my own future is uncertain. If you knew, you would know my weakness."

"Did you claim her against her will?" Dakar asked calmly, as he followed his friend's lead, and tugged his environmental suit on over his clothes.

Torven advanced on him with hands curled into fists. "Never!"

"Of course, you didn't." Dakar walked over and slapped a hand on Torven's back. "You think I don't know that? I know you are an honorable Drexian. I also know you are a passionate one, who is often ruled by his emotions."

"It is my weakness," Torven admitted.

"And also your strength. It makes you a loyal friend and fierce warrior. You would not claim the female if you did not believe she was your mate, and if she was not willing." Dakar shot his friend a look. "Did you really think I would judge you for falling for a female? She is very pretty."

Torven allowed himself a small smile. "She is, isn't she? And she's so soft. Nothing like the aliens on the pleasure plan—"

Dak laughed when his friend stopped talking and color rushed to his face. "It's okay. I know the offerings on the pleasure planets are a weak substitute for a mate." His own smile flickered. "Maybe one day I will be as lucky as you."

"Lucky?" Torven glanced around the cavern. "I'm stranded on a frozen planet and accused of treason. The Kronock are after me, and my mate has run away. What is lucky about this?"

"At least you have a mate. Once we find her, you will explain that you were an idiot. It is not your fault you don't have my natural charm with females."

Torven bristled briefly before nodding. "You are right. I was foolish."

Dakar slapped him on the back again, this time harder. "Of course, you were. I am your best friend, and know this about you. I doubt the female understands your intentions."

"You think she believes I do not care for her?"

"You did a good job of convincing me yesterday. Aside from a lot of hostility on her part, I would not have known you knew each other very well at all." Dakar tapped a finger on his chin. "Although, the hostility from her should have told me she knew you better than you were pretending."

Torven scowled, picked up his friend's pack, and tossed it at him. "Then I must find her so I can convince her otherwise. Since you are so successful with females, tell me what I should say to win her back."

Dakar rubbed his hand down his chin. "My skills lie in enticing females into short-lived liaisons. I've never attempted to use my charms for anything more permanent." He glanced at his friend. "I don't think flowery words will work in this situation, my friend. You need to swallow your pride, tell her the truth, and hope she has a forgiving nature."

Torven scowled. Dakar had always been the fun-loving, ladies' man who could sweet-talk his way out of anything and into any female's heart. He hadn't expected such sober advice, but he knew his friend was right.

Taking a few long steps toward the entrance to the tunnel leading up, Torven paused and looked back. "Are you coming with me?"

Dakar hooked the pack over his shoulder. "To see you grovel at a female's feet? I wouldn't miss it for anything."

CHAPTER TWENTY-FIVE

Trista stumbled on the ice and fell to her knees, cursing as she hit the ground. Snow swirled around her, and tiny ice pellets stung her face, making it hard to see. She pushed herself back up and trudged forward.

She hadn't expected to walk out of the tunnel into a snowstorm, that was for sure. To be honest, she hadn't thought much past the point of storming out of the cavern. Her plan was to stow away on Dakar's ship, but she didn't know where it was or if it was using cloaking technology to shield it from the Kronock. Somehow, she'd imagined that it would be easier to locate his ship, but she'd been walking for what seemed like hours.

She leaned against a frozen boulder to catch her breath, looking behind her at the path that was covered instantly by falling snow. So much for returning to the tunnel and the underground springs. She had zero chance of retracing her steps and returning to Torven. Not that she wanted to.

Despite the frigid temperature, anger flashed hot and fast as she thought back to how he'd acted around his friend. It didn't take a genius to figure out that he hadn't wanted Dakar to know that they'd slept together. Her face burned with familiar humiliation.

And then he expected her to stick around with him and be a fugitive? Well, no thank you. The big jerk could find himself a new doormat.

Trista took a breath. Her lungs were slowly adapting to the thinner air, but she still never felt like she got a full breath on the surface. She wished for a moment she was back in the cavern with the warm, humid air. She recalled splashing in the hot spring with Torven and the way the water looked when it beaded on his muscular chest. Her heart thudded as she remembered how the water looked dripping off the rest of him.

"Stop it," she told herself. "Forget about him."

Easier said than done, she thought as she plodded forward. The path out of the mountain had gotten steeper as she descended. She kept away from the edge, pressing one hand to the rock face so she wouldn't accidentally walk off the cliff.

Rounding a corner, she almost walked into a huge figure. She tried to back away, but tripped, and the creature caught her by the arm. She couldn't see much in the snow, but his grip was tight. Had she walked right into the Kronock?

As he pulled her close, she peered up and recognized the clear face mask. He wore an environmental suit like hers, although his clearly wasn't out of oxygen. For a moment, her heart leaped as she thought Torven had found her, then she focused on the face. It wasn't Torven or Dakar, although she was pretty sure he was Drexian.

She tried to shake him off, but he held tight.

He removed his face mask and hood.

"Who are you?" she asked, warily. She squinted up at him. His brown hair and nearly black eyes looked familiar, but all Drexian warriors were big and brawny, with bronze skin and some shade of brown hair. "I am Karsh. You must be Trista."

"You know me?"

"I was sent to rescue you," he said. "The Drexian empire is very worried about your safety."

Trista couldn't help worrying about Torven. Did this mean they were here to arrest him again?

"How did you find me?" She had to raise her voice to be heard over the storm.

Karsh took her arm and tugged her a few feet until they were under the relative shelter of an overhang in the rock. "We have been searching for you since the traitor Torven kidnapped you from the station."

Trista flinched at his description. As angry as she was with him, she couldn't believe Torven was guilty of committing treason, especially when his friend Dakar believed him, and even Mandy's husband, Dorn, was working to clear his name.

"Where is the criminal?" Karsh asked.

Even if Trista wanted nothing more than to get off the planet and return to the space station, she would not be the reason Torven was captured. She shrugged. "Who knows, and who cares? I hit him on the head with a boulder, and left him for dead."

Karsh's eyes widened, and the corner of his mouth quirked up. "You killed a Drexian warrior?"

"Like you said, he was a criminal, and he kidnapped me."

Karsh released his grip on her arm. "That makes my job easier. Now, I just need to return you to the station."

"Good. I'm dying to get back and have some decent food."

Karsh looked her up and down. "Are you weak? I can carry you."

"No." She waved him off. "I can walk. Actually, if we're heading back to civilization, I can run."

The Drexian laughed. "Come. I will take you back to the civilization you desire."

She followed close behind him as they trekked out of the mountains. In the distance, a geyser of water shot up from the ground, and then another. The ice rumbled gently under her feet. The planet definitely wasn't as placid as it appeared on a first viewing, and she wondered how many more underground caverns were tucked away beneath the surface. Then she thought about their underground cavern and whether Torven had discovered her missing yet.

Not that it mattered, she reminded herself. He didn't need her, and she had no plans to divulge his hiding place, so as far as she was concerned, he was safe and could stay there forever.

Trista focused on the Drexian in front of her. Karsh's environmental suit was as white as the surrounding ice, but he left his hood down, so she focused on keeping his dark hair in view. He was wider than Torven and not as tall, even though he was still well over six feet. His hair was cropped close to his head and he was clean-shaven—definitely not like the rough-around-the-edges Inferno Force warriors she'd met. She wondered if she'd seen Karsh on the Boat before, but if she had, she didn't remember.

They continued walking down into a valley, and Trista scuffed her foot on the ground to see if she was walking on frozen soil or frozen water. No way did she want to take another unplanned dip into an arctic lake.

The Drexian craned his neck around and motioned ahead. "We're almost there."

She peered around him and spotted a black spaceship. It looked larger than the shuttle Torven had commandeered, but she didn't see any other warriors nearby. "Is it just you?"

Karsh nodded. "The fleet sent out lots of ships to search for you, so we couldn't send full crews with each one. Most, like me, came out solo."

"How did you manage to track me down when no one else could?" she asked. "It's not like this planet would have been a natural place to look."

Karsh grinned at her, flashing lots of white teeth. "I guess I got lucky."

Trista thought that was a pretty cagey way not to answer her question, but maybe he figured military strategy was beyond her. She remembered how startled Torven had been, when she'd shown him her mechanical ability. She couldn't help smiling when she remembered that he'd also seemed impressed as he watched her work on their shuttle's damaged engine. She shook her head to get the thoughts of him from her mind.

"Are you unwell?" Karsh asked.

"No, I'm fine," she said, casting a glance over her shoulder at the expanse of white stretching out behind them. "Just glad to put this place in the rearview mirror."

Karsh frowned. "What is a rearview mirror?"

"Nothing. It's an Earth thing."

He shrugged as they reached the ship and he lowered a ramp on the side. Stepping back, he waved her inside and followed behind.

Trista paused once she was on the ship. This vessel was definitely bigger than the shuttle, but the insides were the same shiny black as the exterior.

She watched her environmental suit morph into black and disappear into the background. "You don't mind if I lose this, do you?"

"Of course not." Karsh stepped closer to her and reached for the zipper. "Allow me to assist you."

She moved away from him. "That's okay. I've got it."

His eyes clouded for a moment, then he nodded. "If you do not need my help, I will be in the cockpit."

Trista watched him walk away, an uneasy feeling twisting in the pit of her stomach. A Drexian warrior had been sent to rescue her, so why did the whole thing give her the heebie-jeebies? She should be thrilled to be getting off the uninhabited ice planet and away from Torven, but instead, she felt sick at the thought of leaving him.

Please don't tell me I have that syndrome where kidnapped people fall for their captors, she thought. Stockholm Syndrome, that was it.

"No, it's not Stockholm Syndrome," she whispered, as she stepped out of her dirty, torn suit.

She picked up the heap of fabric and couldn't help remembering Torven offering to switch suits with her when he saw hers was ripped. Then her mind went to their two bodies pressed close together for heat, and the feel of his hard muscles against her. Panic fluttered in her chest. Had she jumped to conclusions because her feelings had been hurt? It wouldn't be the first time she'd acted on a knee-jerk response.

Trista pressed a hand to her chest and could feel her heart knocking against her ribs. She couldn't leave him. Not without talking to him, first.

Glancing up at the cockpit, she wondered how she could get off the ship without her rescuer noticing. She peered around for a way to open the ramp again and finally pressed a flat panel, getting ready to make a run for it as soon as it dropped down.

Instead of the ramp lowering, a door slid open. Trista backed away as the body of a Drexian fell out onto the floor in front of her. She slapped a hand over her mouth to keep from screaming.

"I wish you hadn't done that," Karsh said from behind her.

Trista didn't need to face him to know the sound she heard was a blaster powering up. She squeezed her eyes shut, wishing desperately she'd never run away from Torven.

CHAPTER TWENTY-SIX

Torven put up a hand to shield himself from the biting snow, keeping his eyes on Dakar's head in front of him. His face was numb from the icy air, and ice crystals had formed on his lashes, making it hard to blink.

They'd been searching for what seemed like hours, although he knew his worry made it feel like longer. He hated the thought of Trista out in the storm. He knew she wasn't as fragile as she looked, but he also doubted she was used to surviving harsh climates. At least she had her environmental suit, he reminded himself. And the rations and supplies in the backpack.

He forced down a feeling of panic. Neither of those things would help her if the Kronock found her. His enemy was not known for their kind treatment of prisoners, or for even taking prisoners in the first place. He pushed the thought from his mind, and kept moving forward as the wind howled around him.

This was his fault. If he hadn't been so worried about preserving his honor, she never would have left. He'd been a fool, and he'd hurt her, and now she was wandering around in a blizzard by herself.

"We'll find her," he muttered to himself, his breath warm on his lips. "We have to."

Nothing mattered anymore except finding Trista and keeping her safe. He didn't care about the charges against him, or what people might think of him. He just wanted her back safe in his arms.

Dakar turned and yelled something, as he gestured to a point in the distance. The storm made it impossible for Torven to understand him, but he looked ahead and spotted what had grabbed his friend's attention.

A sleek, black Drexian ship sat in the middle of an open space. From the design, Torven could tell was one of the newer ships, and he was surprised that Dakar had been able to acquisition it for his use. He'd expected his friend to be using the older Inferno Force shuttle they'd traveled from their battleship in. One that did not shine black, and carried the scars from plenty of battles.

As he squinted through the falling snow, Torven saw movement near the ship and recognized two people in Drexian environmental suits, their heads the only thing not blending into the white surroundings. His heart caught in his throat when he realized that Trista was one of them. Her pale hair made his breath hitch in his throat, and it was all he could do not to start running toward her.

Who was she with? He was pretty sure Dakar had not brought a copilot with him. As he watched the Drexian raise his arm and the ramp to the ship lower, it was clear that this was not his friend's ship.

He grabbed Dakar's arm and bellowed over the wind. "Not yours?"

Dakar shook his head vigorously. Torven looked at the vessel again. Had the Drexian hunting parties found him already? It would explain why Trista was with them.

His heart sank as he watched her walk onto the ship. She wasn't being dragged or forced. She was leaving voluntarily. Leaving him voluntarily.

You gave her no reason to stay, he told himself.

He expected her to be upset, but he couldn't help feeling hurt that she had been so eager to abandon him. Maybe she hadn't felt what he had when they'd been together. Perhaps her anger at him was greater than anything else.

Dakar stopped, and Torven almost ran into him. "If they are here to bring you both back, we shouldn't let them see you. Not unless you want to find yourself in custody again."

Torven nodded, although he hated the thought of letting Trista leave without trying to talk to her. But going on the ship to confront her would be the same as turning himself in, and until he was sure that Dorn had evidence proving his innocence, doing that meant he would be convicted of treason.

Dak rested a hand on his arm. "You okay?" he mouthed.

Torven nodded as relief overtook his sadness. At least Trista was going back with Drexians, and would no doubt be returned to the Boat. She hadn't been captured by Kronock or frozen to death. She was safe.

He tried to force the thought that he may never see her again from his mind. As much as he wanted her to stay with him, he knew this was the best thing for her. It was what she wanted. He choked down his disappointment that she hadn't wanted to stay with him. But after how he'd behaved, who could blame her? Torven only hoped he would get the chance to explain what had happened when he was proven innocent.

He held onto his hope of being free again, imagining being reunited with Trista on the Boat. At the moment, it was all he had.

Dakar nudged him. "You ready to go back to the cave, Torv? It looks like she's safe."

Torven nodded but didn't move. He couldn't tear his eyes from the ship she'd vanished into. Knowing she was so close but out of reach was maddening. He knew he was foolish to hope for her to come back out of the ship so he could get a final glimpse, but his feet felt rooted to the ground.

"Did you see other Drexian ships when you arrived?" Torven asked, cupping his hand over his mouth so his friend could hear him.

Another shake of the head from Dak. "Only Kronock. I'm surprised we haven't run into any of them."

Torven peered around him but could see no evidence of his enemy. Had they left the planet and given up their hunt? He doubted it.

The ramp to the Drexian ship lowered again, suddenly, and Dak pulled him down. The two men huddled low to the ground as they watched the other Drexian warrior reappear and stride out of the ship. He looked around, spoke into something on his wrist, and appeared to wait.

"What's he doing?" Dakar asked.

"Waiting for the rest of his team?" Torven suggested. He couldn't imagine the Drexians sending only one warrior in such a large ship.

The wind died down as they waited, the sharp, freezing rain becoming thick flakes of snow that swirled from the sky. Torven's breath was warm as he blew into his hands and kept his eyes trained on the dark hull and the warrior standing outside it.

After a few minutes, a pair of figures appeared from the far side of the ship, approaching from behind a ridge on the opposite side. Torven inhaled sharply. Even though they were far away, he knew instantly they were Kronock from the gray hue of their scaly skin, and the thick legs with clawed feet scraping across the ice.

"Our Drexian brother is going to be ambushed," Torven said, starting to surge to his feet.

Dakar put a warning hand on his shoulder and held him down. "I don't think so."

Both warriors watched in shock as the Drexian walked to greet the two Kronock soldiers. He gave them an abrupt bow before the group conversed for several minutes.

"I don't understand," Torven said in a low voice that shook with anger. "What would a Drexian be doing talking to our sworn enemy?"

They watched as the Kronock walked back in the direction

they'd come from, and the Drexian disappeared into the ship, the ramp closing behind him.

Dak turned toward, him his expression grave. "Isn't it obvious? We've found the real traitor."

The black-hulled ship shuddered as its engines roared to life, snow scattering behind it as it lifted off the ground.

Torven stared at the departing ship, his heart racing. "And he has my mate."

CHAPTER TWENTY-SEVEN

Her head pounded as she came to. Where was she? Trista tried to move her hand up to rub her aching head, but found her wrists were bound behind her back. She swallowed and tasted blood, running her tongue over a cut in her lip.

Panic fluttered in her stomach as she tried to remember what had happened. She'd been on the ship with the other Drexian. What was his name again? Her memories were hazy, but were slowly coming back to her. He'd shot her. She remembered hearing the blaster power up before feeling a blast of heat and collapsing to the floor. That bastard had actually shot her. She touched the tip of her tongue to the tear in her mouth and flinched. That must have been how she'd split her lip.

Anger overtook her panic. She didn't know what was going on, but she knew she had to get out of there. She managed to heave herself upright so she was sitting up with her back against something cold and hard. Swiveling her head, Trista could see that she was sitting in a storage closet of some kind. Metal shelving was soldered to the walls on each side of her with bins stacked high behind steel mesh doors. It looked like someone had stocked the ship for a long trip.

Her stomach churned as she realized the ship was moving. She heard the hum of the engine, and could tell they were flying at a steady speed. Since this ship was larger than the shuttle she'd flown on with Torven, the engines gave off heavier vibrations.

Stay calm, Trista told herself. *If he wanted you dead, he would have killed you instead of stunning you.*

She opened and closed her fists, tugging against her bindings. She wished she could get her hands on a blaster and have a go at the jerk who'd shot her. And kidnapped her. She shook her head. She couldn't believe she'd been kidnapped. Again.

"This is getting a little old," she muttered to herself.

Karsh. That was the name of the Drexian who'd convinced her he was saving her. She could have kicked herself. She'd walked right on board his ship and into his trap, although to be fair to herself, he'd been very convincing. Nothing about his story had seemed off. That is, until she'd happened to find the dead body of a Drexian stashed away in this ship.

Trista felt another stab of panic. She was being held captive by someone who'd killed his own crewmate. That wasn't good. What was to stop him from killing her? She didn't know why he'd taken her, but she now knew it wasn't to rescue her and get her back to the space station. If that had been the case, he wouldn't have needed to get rid of the other guy and subdue her.

She looked around the storage closet more intently now. She had to free herself. No way was she going to go quietly to wherever the hell this guy planned on taking her.

Trista thought of Torven back on the freezing planet and choked back a sob. By now, he and Dakar must have discovered her missing. Had Torven been upset to find her gone? She'd wanted him to feel the sting of her leaving him, but now that seemed terribly petty. All she wanted was to throw herself in his arms and have him tell her he wouldn't let anything happen to her.

She blinked hard, her eyes stinging. Torven wasn't there to save her. She'd made sure of that. The only way she'd probably ever see him again was to get away from Karsh.

Gritting her teeth, she scooted her hands up under herself. She might not be super athletic, but she'd always been flexible. You didn't have to be stick-skinny to be able to do the splits or touch your toes, and she'd spent her childhood mimicking the girls in her neighborhood whose main goal in life was to be a cheerleader. She pulled her bent legs close into her chest, while extending her bound arms. Her wrist bindings dug into her flesh, and she pressed her lips together to keep from crying out in pain. When she'd finally tucked her feet under her wrists, she pulled her arms out in front of her.

She was breathing hard and blood trickled down her arms, but she was pleased with herself. It was definitely easier to move this way. Trista grabbed one of the shelving units and pulled herself up to standing. Scanning the room, she didn't see any way to remove or cut through the hard, plastic ties slicing into her wrists.

Trista pushed against the door and it opened easily. Karsh must not have expected her to wake up or manage to get up. His fault for underestimating her.

She crept out into the central area of the ship. It was empty, so she assumed Karsh had put the dead body back into the closet. She gave an involuntary shudder as she thought about the wide, unseeing eyes of the dead Drexian. That was not going to be her.

The only noises came from the cockpit, so she tiptoed closer. Karsh sat at the pilot's console with his back to her. A loud beep sounded, and he tapped his fingers on the touch screen.

"Incoming transmission," the computer said, the voice female and only slightly stilted.

Karsh let out a huff of breath as he tapped again. "Identify yourself."

"I am Dakar, a warrior of the Drexian Empire and a member of Inferno Force. Who are you, traitor?"

Trista nearly wept at the sound of Dakar's voice. He'd tracked her ship. That meant he and Torven knew she'd been taken and had come after her. Well, she assumed Torven was with him. It could just be his friend who'd come for her. That thought dampened her excitement.

Karsh twitched, clearly not pleased by being called a traitor. "I am not the one wanted by the Empire. That's your friend."

"I saw you talking with the Kronock," Dakar said. "I know it was you who conspired with our enemy, and my Inferno Force brothers will prove it."

Karsh growled and slammed a fist onto the arm of his chair. "It is your word against mine. I am the son of Terk, a member of the High Command. No one will believe you."

Trista watched out the front glass as several Drexian ships materialized in front of the ship, flanking them. They were not as sleek as the one she was in, but they'd obviously been outfitted with stealth technology. Karsh cursed and slowed the engines.

"Tell that to Inferno Force," Dakar said.

Karsh scraped a hand roughly through his short hair. "I have the Earth female. If you want to see her alive, you'll back off."

"You wouldn't dare harm a tribute bride." This voice was not Dakar's. If Trista wasn't mistaken, it was Dorn's. He must be on one of the Inferno Force ships blocking their way.

"Why do I care?" Karsh said. "She isn't my bride. I was denied my bride, or don't you remember, Dorn?'

So Karsh recognized the voice, as well.

"Your own brother stole my bride from me," Karsh continued. "But maybe I should take this one as compensation. I'm sure she'd much rather be mated to me than to a fugitive."

"You will not touch her." Torven's voice was a dangerous rumble as it was projected into the cockpit.

Karsh laughed. "Is that the criminal himself? Perhaps I should summon High Command and claim my bounty."

"You will claim nothing but a jail cell," Torven said.

"Unless I claim your female. I don't suppose you'd like that, would you? She's tied up and unconscious right now, and I can do anything I want with her."

"I would not recommend that," Dakar said, "unless you wish to spend the rest of your life being chased across the galaxy."

Karsh drummed his fingers on the console. "I will give you your precious female, if you give me safe passage away from here."

"You know we cannot let a traitor—" Dorn began.

"Done," Torven's voice cut across his.

Karsh turned his head slightly, and Trista saw the edges of his mouth curl up. "You seem very attached to this female. Maybe I should have a taste of her before I return her. Just to see what all the fuss is about."

The console emitted a series of high-pitched beeps, and Karsh glanced down. "You've locked torpedoes on me? You Inferno Force warriors never could take a joke."

"Prepare to be boarded and prepare to hand over the tribute bride," Dorn said.

"How do I know you won't go back on your part of the bargain?" Karsh asked. "How do I know you'll let me go once you have the female?"

"Are you questioning our honor?" Dakar asked.

"I require an exchange. One of your Inferno Force warriors in place of the female. I will release him on an outpost when I have gotten far enough away."

"You are in no position to bargain," Dorn said.

"I am if you want your female back alive and—" Karsh paused and gave a low laugh "—untouched."

"I will be your hostage," Torven said. "You can take me in her place."

Karsh's smile widened. "This just gets better and better."

Trista's pulse quickened. Torven cared for her enough to sacrifice himself. How could she have ever thought he didn't have feelings for her? But there was no way she was letting him be taken while she went free. She knew there was no point to her being free and returning to the Boat without him.

Looking around her, she spotted Karsh's environmental suit in a pile on the bench seat that ran along the wall behind him. Tucked into the belt of that suit was a blaster.

Moving slowly, Trista picked up the blaster and pointed it at the back of Karsh's head. She checked the settings, considering for a moment if she should move it from stun to kill, but quickly decided she didn't want to add killer to her resume.

"Do you agree to my terms?" Torven asked.

Trista fired before Karsh could answer, and she watched him twitch before collapsing in his seat. She didn't lower the blaster as she stepped closer to the console.

"No deal," she said. "I'm not going anywhere without you."

CHAPTER TWENTY-EIGHT

Torven hovered above the hatch as the Inferno Force shuttle latched on to the Drexian traitor's ship, the sound of the metal clamping to metal making him almost weep with relief. Having to listen to Karsh bargain with his mate's life had been almost too much to withstand, and he'd nearly collapsed when he'd heard the blaster fire.

He knew Trista was fine, she'd told him so over the comms link, but he wouldn't be able to breathe easy until he saw her for himself. The fact that she'd shot Karsh hadn't surprised him, but a part of him wished she had done more than stun him. A traitor who would deign to betray his people to the Kronock deserved nothing less than death.

"Lock complete," Dakar called back from the cockpit.

Torven put his hand to the panel and the round hatch slid open, revealing a smooth black hatch below it. He pounded his hand on the metal, and it opened with a whoosh to reveal Trista peering up at him.

Torven dropped down into her ship and gathered her in his arms in a single motion, clutching her tightly.

"Whoa." She wiggled in his grasp. "What are you doing?"

"You're really all right." He held her out at arm's length, giving her a quick once-over to be sure she was truly unhurt.

She tried to shake him off, but he didn't let go. Her expression was fierce, and she still held the blaster he assumed she'd used to incapacitate Karsh.

Torven was so happy she was safe, he didn't care that the look she gave him was murderous. If it was possible, her anger made her even prettier, giving her cheeks a delicate flush and making her eyes flash.

He reached a hand out to stroke her hair, and she slapped it away. "If you think you can waltz on here and act like nothing happened, then think again, buddy."

"You're upset that I was an idiot," he said.

She stopped struggling. "So, you admit you were a colossal jackass?"

He nodded, bringing a hand to her face and tracing his thumb along her jawline. "Yes. I was so concerned with preserving my honor that I acted stupidly and hurt you. Can you forgive me?"

Her mouth fell open. "I'm not used to guys admitting they were wrong."

"Maybe that's because they didn't love you like I do."

Her mouth dropped even more. "You...you...do?" She met his eyes, blinking away tears. "I thought you didn't care about me."

He bent and brushed his lips over hers. "You are all I care about. You are all that matters to me."

"As crazy as it is, I love you, too." She choked back a sob. "When I heard you volunteer to take my place, the thought of losing you made me crazy. I knew he'd kill you, and I couldn't bear that."

Torven tangled his hand in her hair and pulled her mouth to his, his heart pounding as she kissed him back just as fiercely.

She slapped his chest when he pulled away. "Don't ever do that again."

"Kiss you?" he asked.

"No," she swatted him again. "Sacrifice yourself. No more doing boneheaded things because of your Drexian honor."

"You think saving you was..." he hesitated as he said the word slowly, "boneheaded?"

Trista held up her blaster. "To be clear, I didn't need saving."

He held up his hands in mock surrender. "You are right. Karsh underestimated how formidable you are. Something I plan to never do again. But I can't promise I won't do everything in my power to keep you safe."

She frowned. "I guess that protective thing is baked into your DNA, right?"

Torven swept a loose hair off her forehead. "I know you have been hurt before. I hurt you once. I will spend the rest of my life making sure you're never hurt again."

She let out a shaky breath. "You make it really hard to stay mad at you."

"Would it make you feel better to shoot me again?"

A laugh burst from her lips. "No. I think I've had about enough of shooting people for today."

"Where is the traitor?" Torven asked, letting his gaze leave her face for a moment to scan the interior of the ship.

Trista jerked her head to one side. "I tied him up so he couldn't escape if he came to."

Torven followed the direction of her head and did a double take. The Drexian was indeed tied up, but he was on his side, with his arms and legs bowed behind him and bound together. He appeared to be unconscious, but there was no way he'd be escaping even when he awoke.

"I hog-tied him," Trista explained, smiling at her handiwork.

Torven didn't recognize the warrior, but he knew that he was the son of one of the most powerful members of the High Command, a fact that would do him no good after the truth came out. Torven almost felt bad for the Drexian, knowing that he was about to be branded a traitor. But not quite.

"Now what?" Trista asked.

Torven turned back to her. "Now I take you back home." He took her hands in his. "To our home."

"The charges against you are dropped?"

"They will be, once we turn over Karsh and give the High Command our evidence," Torven said. "Dorn's brother was able to determine that Karsh's father was the one who was behind a recent sabotage operation on the space station, falsifying medical records, and banishing the only doctor who knew the truth."

Trista glanced down at the prisoner. "So, this guy wasn't in it alone?"

"I'm sad to say that a member of our most elite ruling body was also a traitor," Torven said. "He and Karsh were working with the Kronock, and they needed someone to take the fall for it. That's where I came in."

"That's awful, but we have lots of corrupt politicians on Earth so I'm not completely surprised."

Torven frowned. "A corrupt Drexian is very rare. It means you have no honor, and that is a fate worse than death."

"How does it feel to have your honor restored?" Trista asked.

Torven grinned at her. "It feels much better to have you back in my arms."

She looked up at him. "You sure you're not going to change your mind as soon as your friend comes around again?"

Torven's cheeks flamed hot. "I was stupid. I did not want my friend to know I'd claimed you, because it was no longer my right."

She raised an eyebrow. "Your right?"

"Even though we were matched, I lost any claim to you when I was arrested. If I was found guilty, which I would have been, if my friends hadn't uncovered the plot, our bond would have been severed and you would have been matched to another warrior."

She nodded slowly. "So, the fact that we...?"

"Was a violation of my Drexian code," he said.

"And that's why you were so weird when Dak showed up?"

"I know now how wrong it was," Torven said.

"I told him he was an idiot," Dakar called from above, his head hanging down from the open hatch.

Trista grinned up at Torven's friend. "I knew I liked you."

Torven emitted a low growl. "Not too much, I hope."

"Torv," Dakar said. "You're being an idiot again."

Torven pulled Trista into a deep kiss, wrapping his arms around her and lifting her feet off the ground.

When he released her, she gasped for breath. "You're forgiven." She pulled him down so her lips were at his ear. "And you can violate my code anytime you want, big man."

He grinned, feeling a familiar warmth flood his body and his cock harden.

Dakar cleared his throat. "I hate to spoil the moment, but we should get the traitor back to the station."

As if on cue, Karsh began to wake. His eyes opened, and he tugged against his restraints before looking up and seeing Trista and Torven. "Release me at once. My father is on the High Command."

"Not anymore, he's not," Dakar said.

Karsh's face dropped. "What do you mean?"

"Drexians who commit treason with the enemy do not hold seats on the High Command," Torven said, his voice a dangerous rumble.

Karsh struggled fruitlessly, screaming when he realized he couldn't move.

"You need to tell me how to do this 'hog-tying,'" Torven said. "It's very effective."

Dakar dropped down into the ship, casting a murderous look at the prisoner. "Why don't you two take the shuttle, and I'll pilot this criminal back?"

"It would be nice not to have to hear him screaming for the entire trip," Trista said over Karsh's continued bellowing.

Torven bent over and nipped her neck. "The only screams I'm interested in hearing are yours."

Trista's cheeks colored a pretty shade of pink as she looked at Dakar, who was feigning deafness. She swatted playfully at Torven. "What am I going to do with you?"

"Marry me, I hope." Torven took her hand in his and pressing a soft kiss into her palm.

She locked eyes with him, her own blue ones wide. "I thought you'd never ask."

CHAPTER TWENTY-NINE

"I swear you didn't tell me about this." Torven looked up at her, as he floated on his back in the aquamarine water.

Trista stood on the edge of the cave pool in their fantasy suite as she tied the silk belt of her pink shorty robe. The bumpy white walls curved up around the long rectangular pool that extended out into the open air. Beyond the edge of the indoor pool was a vibrant-blue sea that stretched out below to the horizon, and the faint outline of another island in the distance.

Even though she knew it was only a holographic projection, the smell of salt in the air and the sounds drifting up from the Greek market below made it feel real. She gazed down at Torven, his bronze body long and glistening in the water. She knew he was real.

"I forgot to tell you about the cave pool attached to the bedroom?" Trista said. "I must have been distracted by the fact that I was nearly eaten by an albino alligator, almost shot by the Kronock hunting party, and abducted by that awful Drexian."

Torven stood up, his entire upper body out of the water as he walked toward her. "Get in, and I'll distract you with different things."

She glanced over her shoulder, pointedly avoiding staring at the water running in rivulets down his hard body. Since their pool was private and no one could see into their suite, Torven was naked, as he had been pretty much since they'd returned to the space station. Trista let her eyes wander back to him, her mouth going dry when she saw his rigid length barely under the surface of the water.

"We're supposed to have our first couples meeting with Serge and Reina today. They could be here any minute."

"Remind me again who this Serge is."

Trista sighed as she watched him drag his hands through his hair. For a moment she was transported back to the thermal springs, with the eerie blue light bouncing off his chest and the steam rising around him.

"Or have you forgotten as well?" Torven asked her with a wicked smile.

"I haven't forgotten," Trista said, trying to regain her focus. "He's the wedding planner, and he takes his job very seriously. Reina is the one you saw me with the first day you were on the station."

"The Vexling?"

Trista nodded. "She gets very nervous when Serge gets worked up, which is all the time."

"This should be fun," Torven mumbled, crossing his arms over his chest.

"They've already given us three days without interruption," Trista reminded him. "I'm afraid if we wait any longer, Serge will have an aneurysm."

Torven grabbed her by the ankle. "Has it been three days already?"

Trista yelped and tried to pull away from him, but Torven tugged her. "You know it has."

"What is that Earth saying you taught me?" Torven asked, grinning up at her as he grabbed her other leg. "Time flies when you're having fun?"

"Torven!" Trista screamed as he pulled her into the water with him. Her silk robe instantly clung to her skin, the pink fabric becoming diaphanous.

Torven picked her up so her legs were wrapped around his waist. "Now this is more like it."

"Don't you ever get tired?" she asked, wiping droplets of water from her face. She knew the answer to that before she asked it, as he'd been insatiable since the moment they'd set foot in the fantasy suite, dragging her straight to the big, white bed.

"I will never tire of you," he said.

Trista believed him. He'd been focused on nothing but her since they arrived back on the Boat and he'd been proclaimed a hero instead of a traitor. He'd even told the Drexian military they'd need to wait to debrief him, which had garnered them both a few raised eyebrows. Dorn had only been amused and had promised to stall the High Command for as long as he could.

He'd been true to his word. The High Command had not bothered them, and neither had her fellow tribute brides, who Trista knew were dying to hear all the details. No, it was Serge who could no longer be stalled.

"You got me all wet." Trista smacked his arm.

Torven cocked an eyebrow. "Oh, I hope so." He lowered his lips to nuzzle her neck. "I plan to get you much wetter."

"You know that's not what I meant..." She began, but stopped as his thick finger teased her opening.

"No?" Torven slid it inside her. "What did you mean, my little grease monkey?"

She shifted to take him deeper, even as she protested her nickname. "Grease monkey?"

He slid a second finger inside. "You don't like it?" He rotated his fingers. "I can always stop."

She dropped her head back and let out a breathy moan. "Don't you dare. I'll be your little grease monkey." She swiveled her hips and met his gaze. "I'll be whatever you want."

"I want you to be mine forever. That's all." He crushed his

mouth to hers, and she welcomed the feel of his tongue swirling with hers as he moved his fingers inside her. Both his tongue and fingers plundered her, making her heart race and her body burn with need.

When he pulled back, his golden eyes were molten with desire. He let out a deadly growl as he bent and captured a nipple through the pink silk plastered to her skin.

She arched against him, lavishing in the sensation of his warm mouth sucking her through the fabric. "You have me. I'm yours."

He shifted his hand so that his thumb was over her clit and began circling it, as he dragged his fingers in and out. Torven sucked harder as her breathing became ragged.

"Torven." She said his name in a gasp, her legs tightening around his waist. She closed her eyes, feeling nothing but the tremors rocking her body as she clenched around his fingers again and again.

"Come for me, beautiful." His words were a dark purr that made her convulse harder. With him, she felt beautiful and powerful and free. Trista let herself go as her release ripped through her, her cries echoing back to her in the cave.

She held onto Torven's shoulders as her muscles went slack.

"I've got you," he said, lowering them both into the water.

She hitched in a breath as she sagged against his chest, her cheek resting on the hard swell of his muscles. He lowered her a few inches, and his hard cock notched between her ass cheeks.

Looking up, she licked her bottom lip. "That was a nice warm-up."

He ran his hands up her back, pulling the soaking wet silk robe from her skin and tossing it out of the pool. "Well, you are warm."

Trista dropped her legs until they hit the bottom of the pool, standing and turning around so she faced away from him. She reached behind her and took his hands, guiding them up her body until he held her breasts. She arched back and raised one hand to loop around his neck, her fingers finding the hard node at the base.

Torven groaned. He walked her forward toward the edge of the pool that overlooked the ocean. The last foot of the pool extended into the open air and she paused, the sun hitting her shoulders as she looked down to where the deep blue water lapped the shore. She knew their suite was not the only one occupied, and if Trista turned her head, she could see the edge of the neighboring balcony. The thought that someone might walk out and see them sent a thrill through her.

"If I walk any further, someone could see us," she said, her voice trembling.

Torven rubbed her nipples between his fingers, as he used one of his legs to spread hers under the water. "Don't worry. I won't let them watch. Unless you like that?"

She sucked in air as the heat of his cock slid between her legs, shaking her head firmly.

"Does the idea excite you?" His whispered words made her moan out loud, and heat throb between her legs.

She'd never been with someone who made her feel so good. All her self-consciousness seemed to evaporate when he touched her, although she wasn't sure she was ready to put on a sex show. At least, not yet. She tilted her ass up for him and his crown teased her, rubbing through her slick folds. "Of course not," she lied.

"Don't worry, beautiful." His voice was deep and velvety in her ear. "You are only mine. Now and forever."

She leaned back, aching for the feel of him inside her. "Torven, please."

He pressed a wide hand down on her back and leaned her so that her arms were extended out and braced against the rock wall. Need coursed through her, and Trista arched her back, her nipples so hard they ached.

"They may not be able to see me claim you, but they can hear that you are mine." He whispered, grasping her hips and plunging into her.

All her breath escaped her as she took him deep. Even after

riding his cock for days, it took her body a moment to adjust to his size. Trista moved her hips, meeting his thrusts and savoring the feel of being filled by him. She moaned loudly, the sound echoing off the curved walls.

Torven entwined his fingers in her hair with one hand and clutched her hip with the other, his fingers biting into her skin. He dragged his cock out until only his crown was inside her. "You want more?"

"I want all of it." She cried out as he slowly slid back in and his girth stretched her.

"I love watching you take all of me," he said, his voice tight.

She knew he was trying not to lose control with his deep, steady strokes. "And I love riding your huge cock, Torven."

Her words stopped him, then he let out a roar as he hammered into her, his rhythm fierce as she felt his control shatter. As he thrust into her over and over, Trista lost all ability to think. Her mind was a storm of desire and her body burned as she rippled around his cock, water slapping the walls of the pool and spilling over the side. Torven knifed up, giving one final hard thrust and pulsing into her.

She collapsed onto the warm rock wall, and his body covered hers as he sank on top.

"You did that on purpose," he said, gasping for breath.

"Did what?" She rolled her head to look at him. "Talk dirty?"

"Mmm." His cock twitched inside her. "Sometimes I wonder what happened to that frightened girl I kidnapped."

"She's gone," Trista said. Even her short time with Torven had changed her enough that she knew she'd never be that insecure person again. She'd learned to see herself as he saw her, and she'd also learned how to scratch beneath his façade of Drexian honor. "She left with that asshole who was willing to die for his pride."

Torven laughed, his breath warm in her ear. "I do not miss either of them."

Before Trista could agree with him, she heard a series of noises behind them.

"I'm not going in there," a high voice said.

"I've waited long enough. If we don't start on the planning, I'll never get these two down the aisle. I was already robbed of Katie and Zayn's wedding. I will not be cheated again, Reina." Serge stomped into the pool cave as Trista craned her neck to see him.

The Gatazoid wedding planner wore a lavender, three-piece suit with pants that flared at the ankles and purple platform shoes. His hair was also purple, but when he spotted Torven's large naked body cocooning Trista's, it started to flush pink at the roots.

Torven twisted around and straightened up to his full height. "You must be Serge."

Serge's perfectly arched eyebrows shot skyward, and he opened and closed his mouth like a fish searching for water.

Trista put a hand over her mouth to keep from laughing as Torven took huge steps across the pool toward Serge, who looked bolted to the floor.

Serge finally shrieked as Torven reached the shallower end of the pool and his lower body emerged from the water.

Reina ran in with her hands flapping. "What's happening? I knew we shouldn't have come in without permission."

Serge spun around as she rushed in and lost his balance, his arms pinwheeling as he staggered to one side and finally splashed into the pool next to Torven. Spluttering and screaming, his head popped up out of the water, then he went under again.

"I don't think he can swim," Trista yelled at Torven, who reached down and pulled up the flailing wedding planner by the collar, setting him on the side of the pool, coughing and dripping water.

Reina's eyes were even larger than usual as she pressed her hands to her cheeks. She stared down at the soggy little Gatazoid, his now solidly pink hair a wet mop draping over his eyes, and her shoulders began to shake with laughter.

Serge staggered to his feet, swept his hair out of his face, and glared at Reina. "When you get yourself together, I'll be outside."

He clomped out of the cave, leaving puddles behind him with each step.

Reina wiped at her streaming eyes. "That's what he gets for being impatient." She turned and headed for the door, pausing and glancing at Torven quickly over her shoulder. "Thank you. That was the best thing I've seen in years."

Trista waded through the water and wrapped her arms around Torven. "So now you've met the wedding planner."

Torven scooped her up and headed for the pool stairs. "And now he won't be bothering us again for a long time."

EPILOGUE

Dakar straightened the sash crossing his chest and studied himself in the mirror. Dark pants, a matching dark jacket buttoned up to the neck, and a sash sagging from the weight of colorful medals. Rarely did he have an occasion to wear his dress uniform, complete with his sash, and he wanted to make sure he looked good. After all, it wasn't everyday his best friend got married and he served as best man for the wedding.

His brown hair, usually swept up into a messy topknot, was brushed back so it fell smoothly around his neck. He fought the urge to drag his hand through it, as he reminded himself about the terrifying Gatazoid wedding planner. Serge would not be pleased if he appeared at the end of the aisle next to Torven with messy hair. It had been all he could do to keep the enthusiastic little alien from cutting his hair off for the occasion.

"Don't worry," a deep voice said from behind him. "Being best man is easier than being the groom."

Dakar turned and saw Commander Dorn standing at the door. He grinned and waved the former Inferno Force commander inside.

"Come to give me some advice about being best man?" Dakar asked. Since Drexian bonding ceremonies didn't have best men or bridesmaids or any of the other human traditions that were now incorporated into the weddings with tribute brides, Dakar had a tenuous grasp on his role and was glad to see his former superior officer.

Dorn also wore his dress uniform, although he was on leave from Inferno Force to serve on the Drexian High Command, and his usually shaggy, dark hair was slicked back. "Make sure the groom gets to the wedding on time would be my best tip."

Dakar jerked a thumb to one side. "He went to see the bride in her dressing room next door."

Dorn raised an eyebrow and glanced at the wall between the two rooms. "So, does that mean the wedding may be delayed?"

"You would have thought two weeks of them barely leaving their suite would be enough," Dakar said with a grin as he took a few long steps to a sleek white couch in the middle of the room, looked down at his starched uniform, and decided to lean on the arm.

Dorn returned the smile and shrugged. "I am also guilty of being unable to control myself with my bride. Another best man tip is do not get caught behind a tree with your tribute bride between the wedding ceremony and reception."

"A tree?" Dakar asked.

"My brother had a wedding in a holographic winter forest." He shivered as if remembering. "Not the warmest place to be half naked. Serge still won't look at me in the eye."

"The wedding planner caught you?" Dakar laughed. "That shouldn't be a problem for me. I don't have a tribute bride, and I doubt I will anytime soon."

Dorn walked over and adjusted Dakar's sash. "I wouldn't be so sure about that. The High Command is very impressed by your part in bringing the traitors to justice. They are also reeling from the embarrassment that one of their oldest and most powerful members was working with the enemy."

"So, you were able to prove it?"

Dorn nodded, his face becoming solemn. "It was High Commander Tek who was able to bury information and get our doctor sent off the station while his son did the dirty work of meeting with the Kronock and passing them information."

Dakar's blood boiled as he thought of a Drexian warrior betraying his people to their sworn enemy. "Why would they do such a thing?"

Dorn crossed to the standing ebony bar across from the full-length mirror and picked up the bottle of Noovian whiskey, swirling its green contents before pouring some in a pair of glasses. "Unknown to the rest of us, High Commander Tek has hated my house for eons. Apparently, he and my father were rivals as boys, and Tek carried the hatred past my father's death. He also despises the mixing of human and Drexian blood, although he kept that secret. When my brother fell in love with the tribute bride meant for his son, he considered it a personal affront."

Dakar took the glass of whiskey from Dorn. "So why not strike at you or your brother? Why betray his people and set up Torven, especially if he hates humans mating with Drexians anyway?"

Dorn sipped the green liquid. "Even though he believes humans are inferior, they are also the only chance for his line to continue. He blamed the entire High Command for not insisting that my brother's wife accept Karsh, but my brother is too far out of his reach on a military-intelligence mission, otherwise I have no doubt he would have attempted to frame him. Luckily for Kax, his mission is too covert for even the High Command to be told details."

"So Torven was a random choice?" Dakar slugged back his drink and felt the burn all the way down his throat.

"Not random," Dorn said. "He was granted a tribute bride before Karsh. Tek couldn't let that stand. They also needed a scapegoat for their treacherous activities and illegal communications. Once Karsh heard Torven was en route to the Boat, he and his father planted evidence that would lead to your friend's arrest."

Dakar shook his head. "It's hard to imagine a Drexian doing any of this."

"Power corrupted Tek. He'd been sitting untouched on the High Command for so long he lost sight of what the Drexian Empire was about. It seems he passed his entitlement down to his son." Dorn let out a breath. "At least we now know how the Kronock were able to breach our defenses. The enemy should be easier to defeat, now that they don't have inside information."

Dakar crossed to the bar and refilled his glass. "You were lucky your family was unscathed."

Dorn's face contorted for a moment, and then he gulped down the remains of his drink. "We'll have to see about that."

Before Dakar could ask the commander to explain, the door flung open, and Serge barreled into the room, stopping in mid-stride when he realized only Dakar and Dorn were inside. He wore an ice-blue suit with tails, and shiny, navy-blue boots with a significant, chunky heel.

"Where is the groom?" he asked, tapping a silver pen against his clear clipboard.

Dakar cleared his throat. "Torven went to check on the bride."

"Check on the...?" Serge sucked in air then leveled a finger at Dakar. "You, my friend, had one job."

"I can—" Dakar began.

"Too late. Talk to the hand." Serge threw up a palm. "All I know is, I'd better see both of you at the altar in five minutes." With that, he stormed out, slamming the door behind him.

"Talk to the hand?" Dakar said.

"It's human slang," Dorn explained. "Serge loves using Earth expressions. Most of the time he gets them right."

"I guess it's a good thing I haven't been matched with a tribute bride," Dakar said, "because I don't think that guy likes me."

"Serge?" Dorn laughed and slapped him on the back. "He doesn't like anyone on a wedding day. He's too worried about something going wrong. When he's not in a full-fledge panic, he's not a bad little fellow. You won't mind working with him."

"Me? When would I be working with a wedding planner?"

Dorn waggled his eyebrows as he walked to the door. "Like I said, the High Command was impressed by your work, and wants to reward you. Your name has been bumped to the top of the list for a tribute bride."

Dakar's mouth went dry as he watched Dorn leave the room. He was getting a tribute bride? As a third son, he'd been so far down on the list he hadn't held out any hope of being matched.

It was one of the reasons he'd acquired such a reputation as a ladies' man on the pleasure planets and various outposts he'd visited. If you never got a bride, you never needed to worry about being known for seducing alien women. Not that his reputation hadn't gotten him in trouble for other reasons, since not all the women he'd charmed happened to be unattached. He'd never pursued mated females, of course, but they'd never bothered to mention their jealous boyfriends when he was busy sweet-talking them out of their clothes.

Sweat beaded on Dakar's forehead. Being matched to a tribute bride meant one female for the rest of his life. He knew if he took a mate it would be for life, but he'd never imagined it would actually happen. One female? One human female? He'd never even seen one unclothed, although he knew they were softer than Drexians, had two breasts, and no pleasure nodes.

He poured himself another Noovian whiskey and pounded it. Why was he letting this affect him? He threw back his shoulders. He was an Inferno Force warrior who'd survived bloody and vicious battles. Anyway, Torven had been matched and he seemed beyond happy.

Torven. Dakar nearly dropped the glass as he realized he was supposed to be getting his best friend to the ceremony site. Dashing out of the holding room, he practically ran to the room next door.

"Torv!" He banged his fist on the door. "It's time."

After a few seconds, Torven opened the door. His uniform jacket was unbuttoned, revealing the craktow tooth around his neck, and his hair looked like he'd been caught in a Tiburnian windstorm.

"I thought I said I needed a few minutes," Torven said, glancing behind him to where Trista stood, smoothing down her wedding dress and assessing her equally tousled hair in the mirror.

Dakar took him by the arm. "It's been more than a few minutes, my friend. The ceremony is about to begin, and if I don't have you at the end of the aisle on time, your wedding planner's head might fly off his body."

"Is it time?" Trista asked, coming up behind Torven, and slapping him on the arm. "I told you we needed to speed things up."

Torven stared down at her, his expression softening as he cupped her face in his hand. "I thought that was because you were about to—"

"Torven!" She slapped him again, her cheeks filling with color and her eyes darting to Dakar.

Normally, Dakar might enjoy this exchange, but at the moment he needed to get his friend to the wedding on time.

"Trista!"

"There you are!"

The female voices made them all turn to see a trio of women in long, powder-blue dresses hurrying down the hall toward them, holding bunches of white flowers. Dakar felt a measure of relief that he was getting reinforcements in the form of Trista's bridesmaids.

The tallest woman pushed past him, her brown hair swinging as she walked, and she waved her flowers at Trista and Torven. There was the smallest swell of a belly underneath the ribbon belt of her dress. "Serge is starting the line-up."

"Sorry, Mandy," Trista said with an apologetic smile. "We got distracted."

"Girl, we know what you were getting." The woman with light-brown skin and sparkling, hazel eyes gave her an arch smile.

"Bridget!" A third woman with a mass of curly red hair nudged the other bridesmaid. "You don't have to say it out loud."

"Come on, Katie." Bridget waved a hand at Trista's hair. "As if we all don't know."

"As if we all haven't done the same thing," Mandy said, winking at Trista.

"Speak for yourself," Katie said, pivoting to face the other bridesmaids. "Did you both walk down the aisle with 'just been fucked' hair?"

Mandy tapped a finger to her chin. "We do need to do something about the hair. Reina will flip when she sees this."

"When she sees what?" The Vexling's high voice echoed in the curved, white corridor as she approached at a rapid clip, her blue hair bobbing atop her head.

Dakar pulled Torven forward. "That is our cue to leave." He gave the women his most charming smile and a small bow. "Ladies, we will see you at the end of the aisle."

Torven gave Trista a last, longing look, as Dakar tugged him by the sleeve down the hall and they passed Reina, who was wringing her spindly hands.

Dakar knew from the wedding rehearsal the day before that the wedding was being held in the Ocean suite, one of the special environments created for the tribute bride wedding ceremonies. He pulled open the door to reveal the long stretch of sandy beach that led to a sparkling-blue ocean. An arch made entirely of white flowers stood at the end of an aisle marked by glass cylinders that held a large pillar candle burning in each one. There were rows of white, wooden chairs for the guests, and clusters of more white flowers tied to the chairs on the aisle. If the timing went according to Serge's plan—and the holographic program didn't glitch—the sun would set behind the bride and groom right as they said their vows.

A pair of men stood behind a cluster of large metal drums at the back, tapping them and filling the air with strange music, although it seemed to fit the setting. Dakar breathed in the scent of salt and the perfume of the flowers as his bare feet sank into the warm sand. He'd thought it odd when Serge had instructed the bridal party to go barefoot, but now he understood why.

The wedding planner stood just inside the door, and his eyes bugged out when he saw them. "What are you doing here?"

Dakar looked back at the ceremony setup. "Isn't this the right place?"

Serge let out a tortured sigh. "You two are supposed to be in the holding room to the side." He waved to a door at the front of the holodeck and off to the right side. "The florist is waiting for you."

Dakar hoped that didn't mean he and Torven were carrying bunches of flowers. He didn't know much about human wedding traditions, but he'd seen the flowers the bridesmaids had been holding. Maybe the groom and best man also held them.

They ducked into the room, closing the door behind them and muffling the sound of the steel drums.

"It's about time."

It took Dakar's eyes a moment to adjust to the dim lighting after being in the bright sun of the beach environment, but when he finally focused on the voice, he was staring at a human female. "Who are you?"

She held up two single flowers. "I'm with the florist, and I'm here to pin on your boutonnieres."

Dakar didn't know what she meant by 'florist' or 'boutonniere,' but he just nodded. For once, he couldn't think of a charming response.

Torven gave him a curious glance, and then gave the woman a small bow. "I am Torven, the groom."

"I can see that." The woman's dark eyes flashed as she eyed his disheveled hair and uniform. "I'm Ella."

Dakar swallowed hard, even though his throat felt like it was coated with the sand that covered the ceremony floor. He'd seen females from all over the galaxy, but he'd never seen one as striking as the one who was buttoning up Torven's jacket and pinning on his flower.

She had brown hair that spilled across her shoulders in soft waves, and wore black pants that clung tightly to her long legs and a snug, white shirt that showed the outline of her high, round breasts. Dakar had to fight the urge to reach for her when she turned to him.

"You don't need as much work as your friend," Ella said with a smile. "That's good."

"Dakar," he said, his voice cracking. "But my friends call me Dak."

"Like a dock for a boat?" Ella looked up at him from under long, dark lashes as she fastened the flower to his uniform.

He wasn't sure, but he nodded anyway.

Her smile widened. "Hi, Dak."

"You're human," Dakar said, finding his voice.

Ella brushed something off his shoulder and her fingers skimmed his neck. Heat radiated up from where she'd touched him, his face warming.

Ella met his eyes and her smile faltered. "That's right."

He didn't know any human females on the station who weren't tribute brides, and his stomach dropped. "Who is your mate?"

Her eyes flashed. "I'm not a tribute bride."

A door on the opposite side of the room opened, and a dark-skinned man poked his shiny, bald head into the room. "All done, Ella? They're about to start."

"They're all set, Preston," the woman said and walked to the door.

Muffled through the other door, Dakar could hear the processional music they'd rehearsed to, and knew he and Torven needed to start walking to the floral arch. His heart pounded in his chest as he watched her leave, desperately wanting to stop her somehow.

"Wait," he called out. "If you aren't a tribute bride...?"

Ella let out a long breath and turned back to face him. "You've heard of the women who reject their matches, or don't want to become tribute brides?"

Dakar searched his memory, and remembered hearing about these humans who lived on another part of the station. "Yes?"

Ella tossed her hair off her shoulder. "I'm one of those."

Dakar watched her leave the room without another word, and his stomach clenched into a knot. He was finally being matched with a mate for life and it wouldn't be the woman who'd just captured his heart.

Thanks for reading RANSOMED!

If you enjoyed this alien abduction romance, you'll love FORBIDDEN. Ella is no one's tribute bride, especially not the cocky playboy Dakar. Too bad she's the only one he wants. And he's one Drexian warrior who's used to getting what he wants.

> "I love this series! But this is my favorite! I love the chemistry between the two main characters and it is hot!"-Amazon Reviewer

For a sneak peek of FORBIDDEN, turn the page!

This book has been edited and proofed, but typos are like little gremlins that like to sneak in when we're not looking. If you spot a typo, please report it to: tana@tanastone.com

Thank you!!

PREVIEW OF FORBIDDEN —TRIBUTE BRIDES OF THE DREXIAN WARRIORS #5

Chapter 1

Dakar ran a hand up her long leg, the skin smooth and warm beneath his touch. When he reached the curve of her bare ass, he buried his face in her neck and inhaled the sweet scent of her hair. Sliding his fingers down to her wetness, he reveled in her throaty moan.

She shifted on top of him, arching her back and grinding her hips so that his fingers parted her hot folds.

"So wet and ready for me," he whispered, feeling her nipples graze his chest.

Without saying a word, she moved so that his fingers brushed her swollen nub, and she let out a breathy gasp.

Dakar's cock throbbed, but he concentrated on the way her body responded to him—the rapid breathing, the swiveling hips, and the small keening noises. He knew how to give a female pleasure, and more than anything, he wanted to feel this beautiful dark-haired woman come just from his touch.

He swirled his thumb around her little bundle of nerves as he drove a thick finger inside her. Clutching his shoulders, she reared back.

"You're so tight," he said, his voice husky. "Can you take more of me?"

Panting was her only response as he thrust a second finger inside, feeling her tight heat stretch for him. He was desperate to have his cock inside her, but not until he'd made her scream with pleasure. Not until she was crying out his name.

He pumped his fingers as he continued stroking her slick nub. From her jerky movements and her shallow breath, he knew she was close. This was what he loved, feeling women abandon themselves in his arms and under his expert touch. He lived for the moans and the cries and the sweet smell of arousal as he touched and licked and fucked them until they screamed his name over and over. Seeing the sated look on their faces made it even sweeter when he finally did bury his cock in them.

"Dakar!" she cried, her voice high and breathy as she met each of his thrusts with one of her own.

Her wavy hair was a curtain around his face, so he couldn't see her expression as she bucked against him, her core clenching his fingers. She cried his name again before collapsing on him, her sweaty body sliding on his and her soft breasts pressing against his hard chest muscles.

He let her breathe for a few moments, before grabbing her by the waist and flipping her on her back. She let out a small squeal, but her legs fell open for him. Blood pounded in his ears as he notched his aching cock between her thighs. The raised nodes on his spine were hard and throbbing, as was his cock. This was what he'd wanted since he first laid eyes on her. The need to claim her was all consuming—it was all he'd thought about in weeks—and now she would finally be his.

"Dakar!"

Her voice was all wrong. It was too low. And what was that pounding noise?

He blinked a few times and his eyes focused on the faint light illuminating his officers' quarters. The window that took up one wall looked out onto an array of stars glittering against the blackness of space, and he saw that the lights inset in the ceiling and walls were slowly illuminating. He remembered that he'd set the lights to mimic a sunrise, so this was his gradual way-up call. He glanced down and saw that he was in bed alone.

"*Grek*," he cursed. Another dream. He kicked off the sweaty sheets tangled around his legs and sat up. The pounding came from the door.

He let out a fresh torrent of Drexian curses as he stood, wrapping the gunmetal gray sheet around his waist and walking to the door. Waving a hand across a flat panel, he frowned as the door opened and revealed his best friend and fellow Inferno Force warrior, Torven.

Torven stood slightly taller than him, but both men shared the wild hair and tattoos favored by Inferno Force, not to mention the broad shoulders and muscular physique of all Drexian warriors. Torven looked him up and down and grinned. "Normally I'd assume you'd had a busy night with a female but we aren't on a pleasure planet or a questionable outpost."

"Don't remind me," Dakar said, scraping a hand through his shaggy, dark hair and pulling it up into his usual topknot.

They were far from both their Inferno Force battleship on the outskirts of the galaxy and the usual places the warriors went for recreation. The Love Boat was neither of these.

Designed as a holographic enticement for humans, the high-tech space station tucked away behind one of Saturn's moons didn't have the willing alien females or nonexistent rules Dakar was used to. As a matter of fact, the Boat was all about rules. It had to be, since this was where human women were brought when they were abducted from Earth to be mated to Drexian warriors.

Dakar had never given much thought to the tribute bride program since, until recently, his chance of being matched was slim.

Like all Drexians, he knew it had started when his people had stopped producing females and were in desperate need of a compatible species. They'd happened upon Earth around the same time a violent race of aliens called the Kronock had attempted to invade it. The Drexians had defended Earth and then made a bargain with the planet. They would keep Earth safe if they could take a select number of females to mate with their warriors and help continue the species.

The deal had been kept secret from all but a few in the Earth's government officials, and the Drexians quietly went about taking females who were compatible—only about half of the human women were—and who had no strong social ties. The tribute brides were brought to the Boat where they were given a holographic fantasy suite and assigned a wedding planner and a special liaison. Most women warmed up to idea once they saw the hunky Drexians and realized there was no option to return to Earth. It didn't hurt that they were wined and dined and treated like goddesses, which was a significant upgrade for most of the women who were taken.

Since the Drexians were limited in the number of women they could take at once, there was a waiting list for brides and priority was given to only sons or warriors from elite families. As a third son, Dakar hadn't expected his name to come up for years, but his recent assistance in retrieving a tribute bride and revealing a mole in the Drexian High Command had gotten him a bump up on the list. Now he was waiting on the station for the next available tribute.

Dakar hated waiting, and he'd been having second thoughts about taking a tribute bride. Especially after he'd met a particularly striking human at Torven's wedding and hadn't been able to rid his mind of her since. He grunted and turned on his heels.

Torven followed him back inside the room. "You look like hell, Dak. You want to tell me what's going on?"

Dakar glanced back at his friend. Thick swaths of black ink swirled down from underneath the warrior's tight black T-shirt and a sharp craktow tooth dangled in the hollow of his neck. Dakar had been with Torven when they'd taken down the deadly craktow. The two had been together for most of their greatest battles. And now they were cooling their heels on a sleek space station that looked nothing like their battleship.

"You know I don't do well when I'm bored," Dakar said. No way was he telling his friend about the dreams. Not when he knew how wrong they were.

Torven grunted in acknowledgment. "Once High Command has determined that the Kronock infiltration didn't go any further, they'll resume the transport of tribute brides."

"How is High Command investigating if their council was the thing that was infiltrated?" The news that one of the long-standing elite families had been working with the Kronock to sabotage the Boat and weaken the Drexian defenses had come as a blow, and the empire was still reeling. The father and son had been taken into custody and awaited trial for treason, a trial and verdict Dakar knew would be swift and final.

"High Commander Dorn is leading the inquiry along with his brother, Kax," Torven said. "Since Dorn is a new member of the council and his brother recently left the governing body to rejoin military intelligence, they have enough distance from the situation to get to the bottom of it."

Dakar nodded. Dorn was also a member of Inferno Force and had been their commander. He knew there was no warrior more fair.

"Is this really about being bored?" Torven asked. "We've gone through long stretches without battle, although I know it's been four weeks already and that's the longest you've gone without some sort of feminine distraction."

Dakar tried to muster a grin. He knew his reputation as a ladies' man had been established long ago, and for good reason. Dakar had always taken great enjoyment in the company of females. Any type of females. He considered it a personal challenge to figure out how to pleasure each species. The pleasure houses had even go so far as to compete for his visits, as he left their females so happy.

"I know there aren't really any options here," Torven continued. "All the humans are matched to warriors and there aren't many other female aliens except the Vexlings and a few others. If I remember correctly, you aren't a fan of those bony creatures."

Dakar rolled his eyes at Torven. "You make it sound like I can't survive without bedding a female."

Torven cleared his throat. "Some of us burned off energy on the hover ball courts or in the fighting rings. You burned off your energy in other ways."

Dakar didn't argue with Torven. He supposed the Drexian was right. He'd been restless since he'd arrived on the Boat. It hadn't helped that he couldn't get the human out of his thoughts. "What do you know about the other humans? The ones who refuse to become tribute brides?"

Torven leaned against the ebony dresser and crossed his arms. "Not much. They live together in special quarters. I think some of them work around the station." He cocked an eyebrow. "Is this about that pretty woman who pinned on our flowers at my wedding?"

Dakar turned from Torven, dropping his sheet and striding naked toward the bathroom. "What woman? I'm just curious."

"They may not be tribute brides anymore, but you know they're off-limits," his friend called to him.

Dakar remembered some sort of warning regarding the former tributes. He guessed the theory was if they don't want to commit to being a tribute bride they didn't get to enjoy the benefits—big, muscular warriors being one of those benefits. It was also why they didn't live in holographic suites that looked like overwater South Pacific bungalows or romantic ski chalets in the Alps or have all their meals delivered. Those perks were saved for the tribute brides who took a Drexian mate.

He leaned both hands on the dark marble sink and stared at

himself in the mirror. The dark circles under his eyes and the heavier-than-usual stubble on his cheeks made him look less like his charming self and more like the dark and deadly friend waiting for him in his room. His gaze dropped to the tattoos that swirled red across one arm and half of his chest—the marks that represented his eternal loyalty to Inferno Force. What he wouldn't give to be back on his battleship and with his Inferno Force brethren and away from temptation.

"Get it together," he told himself. He needed to stop dreaming about the woman he'd met at Torven's wedding, the dark-haired beauty named Ella who'd rejected the idea of being a tribute bride and now lived on the other side of the station.

Torven was right. He needed to forget her and the jolt he'd felt when she'd touched him—like nothing he'd ever experienced before. She could never be his, and fantasizing about her was doing nothing but driving him mad. He squeezed his eyes shut and groaned as an image of her long, wavy hair rushed into his mind. His cock swelled as he imagined the feel of her hair brushing against his nodes and making them heat.

Easier said than done.

~

To order FORBIDDEN, book 5 in the Tribute Brides of the Drexian Warriors series, click HERE!

Get this free bonus story by clicking below (but I suggest you read TAMED before reading the bonus wedding story)!

BookHip.com/CRJHNH

PREVIEW OF BOUNTY—BARBARIANS OF THE SAND PLANET #1

Below is a sample of another Tana Stone sci-fi-romance series—this one with alien barbarians and female bounty hunters!

Chapter One

"Are they shooting at us?" Danica asked, grabbing the edge of a smooth, metal console as she stepped onto the bridge and the ship heaved to one side. She tasted blood as she bit the inside of her mouth, and flinched from the pain. *Son of a bitch.*

She and Bexli had just brought their latest captive onboard, and she'd given the order to take off, hoping the rival bounty hunters who'd also been in pursuit hadn't seen them. From the staccato sounds of gunfire, she guessed that her plan of slipping out unnoticed was shot to hell.

She took in the familiar sight of the compact bridge—a round, flat panel console in the center of the room with view screens suspended above it, smaller individual consoles forming a half moon around the main one, and a final ring of screened consoles against the circular walls. A long, narrow slit of a window gave them a view out the front of the ship, but had a steel shade they could lower for security. Nearly every part of the room was composed of metal that was long past gleaming, and looked nearly black with age and grime. Wires spilled from underneath most of the consoles, a result of various hacks and patches to keep the aging space ship running. Danica inhaled the scent of burning fuel that seemed to permeate the ship, and felt a rush of affection for the bucket of bolts she'd practically grown up on.

"Looks like it," her pilot, Caro, said turning from one of the smaller consoles where she navigated the ship, her straight, nearly black hair flying behind her as she spun back around. "And we're definitely outgunned."

"Can we outrun them?" Danica asked, as she made her way down to the center console and looked out at the massive ship blocking their escape.

"What we don't have in size or gun power, we make up for in maneuverability," Caro said. "I should be able to get a little extra acceleration from our impulse drives if I boost the—"

"Caro," Danica said, cutting off the woman before she launched into an overly detailed explanation of their engine.

"Sorry, Captain," Caro said spinning back around to her console. "On it."

"I hope you're right," Tori said from where she stood at the weapons console along the wall, her curly, dark hair pulled up in a topknot and held in place with what looked like metal chopsticks with dangerously sharp ends—almost as sharp as her pointy teeth. A row of hard, raised bumps ran above her eyebrows, down along the sides of her face and disappeared into her hairline—a hallmark of the Zevrians—making her look even fiercer than she was. "Because we're running low on weapons."

"How low?" Danica gripped the console with both hands as the ship jerked to the right and skirted underneath the larger ship.

"How good are you at hand-to-hand combat?" Tori asked, her brown, muscled arms braced against the wall.

Danica had gotten a lot of flak—mostly from her father's old bounty-hunter friends—when she'd brought on the Zevrian as her security chief, but she'd never had a moment's regret for making Tori a part of her team. Especially in situations like these.

"I thought we were supposed to stock up when we were docked at Centuri Twelve," Danica shouted over the roar of the engines firing.

"I would have, if we had anything to buy them with," Tori said as the ship accelerated.

Danica sighed. Her crew had been running on fumes—sometimes literally—for weeks. "I know it's been tight, but once we turn over this bounty, we'll be flush for a while."

"I'm just glad Mourad won't have the satisfaction of beating us." Caro turned to face forward as the force of acceleration pressed her back into her chair. "I hate that guy."

Danica couldn't agree more. The ship shooting at them belonged to a bounty hunter and mercenary named Mourad, who didn't believe in female bounty hunters and didn't believe in playing fair. Not that Danica was against stretching the rules or pushing her luck, but Mourad had no limits on what he and his crew would do to capture a bounty.

He was the one bounty hunter her father had gone out of his way to avoid, because Mourad ignored all the usual professional courtesies and accepted practices. He would double-cross anyone. Instead of tracking down bounties himself, he was known for waiting until another bounty hunter did all the legwork, then he and his band of mercenaries would swoop in and snake the bounty. Just like he was trying to do now.

Over my dead body, Danica thought, as their ship broke through the atmosphere and shot into space, the sky going from hazy yellow to inky blue to black. She thumped the side of the console, mentally thanking the ship for getting her out of yet another scrape.

When her father died, he'd left everything to her, which meant basically his ship. It had just been the three of them for as long as Danica could remember—her and her father and the ship. Different crews had come and gone, but the ship had been the only constant in their lives, aside from each other. She'd thought about selling it, but only for a moment. The old ship was as much a part of her as her father had been, and she couldn't stand the thought of losing both of them.

She knew her father had never wanted her to take over his bounty-hunting business. Truth be told, he never thought it was possible, but after spending a childhood chasing after crooks all over the galaxy, she didn't really know any other life. She was good at tracking people and getting out of scrapes and skirting the law. Her father had taught her well.

Danica shook thoughts of her father out of her head as she glanced at the fuel gauge. "Good work. We should have enough steam to reach the Gendarvian outpost, where we can unload our bounty and get our reward."

Tori crossed the bridge to stand next to her, the chain belt wrapped several times around her waist jingling as she walked. "I wonder what this one did to command such a high price."

Danica shrugged, tucking a loose strand of wavy, blonde hair behind her ear. "It's not our business to wonder why. I can tell you it wasn't for a violent offense. I've never had a bounty put up less of a fight."

"The tracking was the hard part. Dr. Max Dryden did a fucking brilliant job of hiding."

The women turned to see their engineer, Holly, step onto the bridge. While the rest of Danica's crew favored utilitarian clothes that made them look more like their male counterparts—military issue pants, T-shirts, multi-pocketed vests and jackets—the ship's engineer and resident computer whiz wore color and patterns and combined them fearlessly. Red hair spilled over her shoulders and down the skintight, pink-paisley top she'd paired over an equally snug pair of turquoise pants. Her decidedly feminine appearance didn't do a thing to stop her from cursing like a space pirate, which usually startled people who thought her girly looks meant she was all sugar and spice.

"Not good enough to outfox us," Tori said, hand on her hip.

"Luckily for you, I understand the doctor's research and narrowed it down to the few planets that are ideal for that type of scientific study," Holly said. “And then Bexli did her thing.”

Bexli was the other non-human in the crew. A Lycithian shape-shifter who excelled at sneaking in and out of otherwise impenetrable places, she was their ace in the hole. Officially, she was their acquisitions officer, but only in the sense that she could acquire any bounty by way of her shape-shifting skills. She was so indispensable, Danica even put up with the pet glurkin that Bexli had insisted on bringing on board.

"Remind me again what type of research," Tori said, then shook her head. "Never mind, I actually don't care."

Holly rolled her eyes at Tori. "The study of a rare mineral only found in a few systems. Word on the astronet is that the doctor has figured out a way to harness its power, which would be fucking amazing."

Caro twisted in her chair to face them. "I'm still not thrilled we're turning over a scientist. Are we sure this is a legit bounty? How many doctors do you know who commit crimes severe enough to command this amount? Should we really be turning in other women? I mean, we’re an all female bounty-hunting crew."

Danica frowned, partly at Caro’s barrage of questions and partly because she'd had the same thoughts, and had been trying to ignore her inner voice during the entire search. "We don't have the luxury of picking and choosing our bounties. Anyway, if we don't turn the doctor in, someone else will. At least we treat our prisoners well."

"Not that all of them deserve it." Tori pulled up the hem of her black cargo pants to reveal a thin, red scar running up her calf. "We should have put that Daxian smuggler out the airlock."

“Agreed,” Bexli said, as she joined the other women on the

bridge, a tiny puff of green fur running along beside her. “He was particularly repulsive.”

“Is the bounty all settled?” Danica asked.

Bexli nodded, and her iridescent-lavender bob swung at her jawbone. “This one was a breeze. I didn’t even have to transform into something terrifying to keep her in line.”

She leaned against a console and scooped Pog up in one arm, ruffling its fur and making it emit a low purr. “The Daxian from our last mission only stopped struggling when I morphed into a gorvon.”

“Remind me again, what’s a gorvon?” Holly asked.

“A particularly gruesome creature from the Daxian’s home world.” Bexli grinned. “Lots of claws and fangs.”

Caro laughed, tightening her high ponytail. “That explains why he soiled his cell.”

"At least he kept us in fuel and rations for a month," Danica said, glancing at Tori. "And you gave him a few scars, if I remember correctly."

Tori grinned. "A souvenir from the bounty hunter babes."

"You know I hate that nickname." Danica folded her arms across her chest.

"Babes is better than the other name they call us that also starts with a *b*." Holly leaned against one of the consoles, crossing her long legs at the ankles.

"I don't mind the name so much," Caro said. "At least they're talking about us."

Danica let out a long breath. "They should be talking about us because we've brought in the two highest bounties in the past astro-year, not because we're all women."

Holly patted her on the shoulder. "It's just because we're the first—and so far only—all-female bounty-hunter crew. Once the novelty wears off, or another crew comes along, people will talk about something else."

Danica knew there was truth in Holly's words, but she hated the fact that even though they'd brought in two of the toughest bounties around, the other hunters still didn't respect them. She'd known working in a field known for tough guys wouldn't be easy, but she'd hoped her unorthodox methods and maverick crew would win her respect. So far, they'd only managed to acquire nicknames.

"I say we own it," Tori said, taking one of the pointy chopsticks from her hair and pressing the needle-like point into the pad of her finger. "We know we can do any job the boys can do and, once we bring in this hot-shot doctor, we'll be rolling in enough dough to outfit this ship so we can blast anyone out of the sky. Let them call us babes then."

"Um, guys." Caro's fingers flew across the screen in front of her. "We probably shouldn't count our money quite yet."

Danica jerked her head to the screens above her, slamming her palm against the console when she saw the rival ship closing in on them. "I thought we had enough of a head start to lose them."

"They're faster than I expected for a ship that large," Caro said, maneuvering their ship so that it dipped to the left.

Holly slid onto the floor, landing with a thud. "A little warning next time."

"Sorry," Caro shouted over the sound of weapons fire hitting their hull. "You should probably brace for impact."

A blast shook the ship and alarms began screaming, red lights flashing overhead.

"Was that a torpedo?" Danica asked, shaking her head in disbelief. Was a rival bounty hunter really trying to blow up her ship?

“Shit.” Holly scrambled to her feet, using the nearest console to pull herself toward the door. "I'd better get back to the engine room. If we lose that, we're dead in the water."

“I'll go make sure the prisoner is okay,” Bexli said, following Holly with Pog tucked under one arm.

The entire ship jolted, and Danica heard the sound of metal scraping against metal. Her skin went cold. "They've clamped on."

Tori's face was grim. "They're boarding us."

"Maybe they'll take the doctor and go," Caro said, although her voice quivered. Danica knew her pilot had been captured more than once when she was a pilot for a resistance movement, and she suspected it hadn't always been pleasant.

Danica squeezed her hands into fists. "They're not taking our bounty or us." She turned to Tori. "Hold them off as long as you can, but don't get yourself killed. I have a plan."

Tori pulled the other chopstick from her hair and slipped both sharp metal sticks into her chain belt. "You got it, Captain."

Danica ran off the bridge and down the dimly lit corridor until she reached a steel door where Bexli stood guard. "I've got the doctor. Why don't you and Pog try to hold off Mourad's soldiers?"

Bexli nodded, her lithe frame and lavender hair transforming into a hulking beast covered in matted fur, with only the slightest hint of purple at the tips. Pog gave a gruff bark and became a green lizard the size of a human, with short legs that scampered across the floor. Both creatures hurried off toward the noise of the enemy bounty hunters boarding their ship.

Danica turned back to the steel door and punched in a code. The door slid open with a groan, revealing a petite figure with short, chocolate-brown hair sitting on the edge of a cot in the sparse room.

"Doctor Dryden," Danica said, her breath ragged. "Some pretty nasty bounty hunters are coming on board to take you. I can promise you they won't be as humane as we've been, but I have a plan that could save us both."

The woman on the cot blinked her wide, blue eyes a few times before answering. "Call me Max."

To be continued . . .

Want to read BOUNTY, book 1 in the Barbarians of the Sand Planet series? Click HERE to keep reading!

ALSO BY TANA STONE

The Tribute Brides of the Drexian Warriors Series:

TAMED (also available in AUDIO)

SEIZED (also available in AUDIO)

EXPOSED (also available in AUDIO)

RANSOMED (also available in AUDIO)

FORBIDDEN (also available in AUDIO)

BOUND (also available in AUDIO)

JINGLED (A Holiday Novella) (also in AUDIO)

CRAVED (also available in AUDIO)

STOLEN (also available in AUDIO)

SCARRED (also available in AUDIO)

ALIEN & MONSTER ONE-SHOTS:

ROGUE (also available in AUDIO)

VIXIN: STRANDED WITH AN ALIEN

SLIPPERY WHEN YETI

CHRISTMAS WITH AN ALIEN

YOOL

Raider Warlords of the Vandar Series:

POSSESSED (also available in AUDIO)

PLUNDERED (also available in AUDIO)

PILLAGED (also available in AUDIO)

PURSUED (also available in AUDIO)

PUNISHED (also available on AUDIO)

PROVOKED (also available in AUDIO)

PRODIGAL (also available in AUDIO)

PRISONER

PROTECTOR

PRINCE

The Barbarians of the Sand Planet Series:

BOUNTY (also available in AUDIO)

CAPTIVE (also available in AUDIO)

TORMENT (also available on AUDIO)

TRIBUTE (also available as AUDIO)

SAVAGE (also available in AUDIO)

CLAIM (also available on AUDIO)

CHERISH: A Holiday Baby Short (also available on AUDIO)

PRIZE (also available on AUDIO)

SECRET

RESCUE (appearing first in PETS IN SPACE #8)

Inferno Force of the Drexian Warriors:

IGNITE (also available on AUDIO)

SCORCH (also available on AUDIO)

BURN (also available on AUDIO)

BLAZE (also available on AUDIO)

FLAME (also available on AUDIO)

COMBUST

THE SKY CLAN OF THE TAORI:

SUBMIT (also available in AUDIO)

STALK (also available on AUDIO)

SEDUCE (also available on AUDIO)

SUBDUE

STORM

All the TANA STONE books available as audiobooks!

INFERNO FORCE OF THE DREXIAN WARRIORS:

IGNITE on AUDIBLE

SCORCH on AUDIBLE

BURN on AUDIBLE

BLAZE on AUDIBLE

FLAME on AUDIBLE

RAIDER WARLORDS OF THE VANDAR:

POSSESSED on AUDIBLE

PLUNDERED on AUDIBLE

PILLAGED on AUDIBLE

PURSUED on AUDIBLE

PUNISHED on AUDIBLE

PROVOKED on AUDIBLE

BARBARIANS OF THE SAND PLANET

BOUNTY on AUDIBLE

CAPTIVE on AUDIBLE

TORMENT on AUDIBLE

TRIBUTE on AUDIBLE

SAVAGE on AUDIBLE

CLAIM on AUDIBLE

CHERISH on AUDIBLE

TRIBUTE BRIDES OF THE DREXIAN WARRIORS

TAMED on AUDIBLE

SEIZED on AUDIBLE

EXPOSED on AUDIBLE

RANSOMED on AUDIBLE

FORBIDDEN on AUDIBLE

BOUND on AUDIBLE

JINGLED on AUDIBLE

CRAVED on AUDIBLE

STOLEN on AUDIBLE

SCARRED on AUDIBLE

SKY CLAN OF THE TAORI

SUBMIT on AUDIBLE

STALK on AUDIBLE

SEDUCE on AUDIBLE

ABOUT THE AUTHOR

Tana Stone is a USA Today bestselling sci-fi romance author who loves sexy aliens and independent heroines. Her favorite superhero is Thor (with Aquaman a close second because, well, Jason Momoa), her favorite dessert is key lime pie (okay, fine, *all* pie), and she loves Star Wars and Star Trek equally. She still laments the loss of *Firefly*.

She has one husband, two teenagers, and two neurotic cats. She sometimes wishes she could teleport to a holographic space station like the one in her tribute brides series (or maybe vacation at the oasis with the sand planet barbarians). :-)

She loves hearing from readers! Email her any questions or comments at tana@tanastone.com.

Want to join her VIP Readers list and be the first to know about contests and giveaways? Click here: BookHip.com/CRJHNH

Want to hang out with Tana in her private Facebook group? Join on all the fun at: https://www.facebook.com/groups/tanastonestributes/

facebook.com/tanastoneauthor

instagram.com/tanastoneauthor

bookbub.com/authors/tana-stone

Cover Design by Croco Designs

Editing by Tanya Saari

Printed in Dunstable, United Kingdom

66811164R00119